heaven
at SEVEN

DONNA EDEN VINKE

heaven at SEVEN

TATE PUBLISHING & *Enterprises*

Published by Tate Publishing & Enterprises, LLC
127 E. Trade Center Terrace | Mustang, Oklahoma 73064 USA
1.888.361.9473 | www.tatepublishing.com

Tate Publishing is committed to excellence in the publishing industry. The company reflects the philosophy established by the founders, based on Psalm 68:11,
"The Lord gave the word and great was the company of those who published it."

Book design copyright © 2009 by Tate Publishing, LLC. All rights reserved.
Cover design by Amber Lee
Interior design by Jeff Fisher

Published in the United States of America

ISBN: 978-1-60799-639-2
1. Fiction, Christian, General
2. Religion, Christian Life, Inspirational
09.06.25

Dedication

To my wonderful children,

Joe, Kevin, Lynn Ann,
Carol Ann, Johnny, and Jeanne.
And to my extraordinary grandchildren,
Nicole, Brandon, Terri, Corie, Aleea,
Cole, Sierra, Chase, and Christian.

Family means putting your arms around each other
and being there.

—Barbara Bush

Acknowledgments

Without the kindness and expertise of my friend, Jim Riordan, I would still be trying to figure out in what tense to write a fiction book. Thank you, Jim, for your patience, your wise and truthful mentoring, and your many prayers.

To my son-in-law, the computer genius, thanks, Kent, for your determination in answering my screwball questions. And thank you Carol for hours of dialogue!

I thank my husband and my children. They have all given their loving support to realize my dream.

To all of the wonderful authors who have inspired me with their books on angels and heaven, especially Joni Eareckson Tada, C.S. Lewis, Randy Alcorn, and David Jeremiah; I'm very grateful.

Thanks to Janey Hays for saying yes, and to the entire staff at Tate Publishing, thanks for your support.

In addition to all of these wonderful people, I thank God the Father, God the Son, and God the Holy Spirit for giving me the love and passion to write what was planted in my heart. I could never have written this story without my favorite book, the Bible.

And last but certainly not least, I thank all those who are about to read this small book. My prayer for each of you is that you recognize heaven is a real place. And heaven is precisely where you want to spend your eternity.

No love, no friendship can cross the path of our destiny without leaving some mark on it forever.

—Francois Mauriac

Table of Contents

Foreword

As a parent who lost a child, I can truthfully say the only real comfort is knowing the soul life of that child goes on. But, other than knowing this soul life includes everything you loved about that child and that some-day you will be reunited for eternity, there is a lot of gray area in such a supposition. *What are they doing?* Yes, I know the Bible says they are infinitely happy, but what does that mean? Surely they don't sit in a vacuum like blessed-out drones. There must be activ-ity, but what kind of activity?

This great little book provides answers to those questions and a great many more. Entirely scriptural and biblically accurate from start to finish, the story is of great comfort to parents like me. It provides a glimpse into heaven through a child's eyes. As a writer myself, I have been blessed with a great imagination—something I have drawn upon many times to get me through the sad days when I miss Jeremiah so much I could just explode. Often, I have felt pity for those poor parents who have not been blessed with the abil-ity to visualize life on another plain. For them, this book is a Godsend.

Within these pages, heaven comes alive! Anyone who has ever thought of the glorious home of God as being a bunch of clouds and violins will be pleasantly surprised to see that it is a place of not only great joy but great events, great friends, and great times. How could it be otherwise? I am blessed to have read these pages, and you will be too!

—James Riordan

James Riordan is the author of *Break On Through: The Life & Death of Jim Morrison*, *The Bishop of Rwanda*, *Madman in the Gate (Songs & Poems About Trying to Live the Truth)*, and others

Winner of twelve national awards

Midwest/Chicago Emmy nominee for writing *Kankakee Valley Prime Time*

Introduction

For as the heaven is high above the earth, so great is his mercy toward them that trust him.

Psalm 103:11 KJV

Have you ever wondered what heaven is like? Heaven is the perfect state. It is a place where we love one another with every fiber of our beings. In heaven, no one is abandoned. There is no rejection, no pain, no suffering, and no sorrow. It is a place of acceptance, where you never say good-bye.

Have you ever wondered where heaven is? If you look at a world atlas, you will find one hundred and ninety-two countries on earth. You can locate countries on seven different continents by something called longitude and latitude, with point zero being in the center of the earth. Every country has its own individual name and place.

Earth is a colossal world, but heaven cannot be found on any earthly map because heaven is not located on earth. Heaven, just like earth, is the work of God's finger. It is the firmament, the atmosphere, and the space beyond the clouds, the moon, the stars, and the sun.

It is the abode of God himself and is beyond our full understanding. Earth has the shape of a circle, and the new earth, which is the eternal heaven, is the circle that goes on and on for eternity.

Heaven is a place of complete wonder and beauty. A place filled with passion and joy. A place of absolute truth that never ends.

———————————

But my life is worth nothing unless I use it for doing the work assigned me by the Lord Jesus—the work of telling others the good news about God's wonderful kindness and love.

Acts 20:24 NLT

As the train traveled upward along the tracks of the narrow path, I remember looking out the window on the side of the railing. Below us, wide curves disappeared into round deep clefts in the rocks. Huge boulders stacked one on top of the other had formed together by the spoken word of God. Like the stroke of a paintbrush, each layer of red, brown, and purple lined up perfectly painted into the side of the mountain. I could hear the wind singing between the peaks of the rocks.

When I looked up, the clouds seemed as if a hidden hand had connected them into rows of big white balls of fluff. We were almost to the top of this wondrous mountain when the clouds began soaring to greater heights, and areas of blue appeared between them. It was like taking a ride to a magic land. The mountain was so big! And the sky so wide!

I thought of God and how great he really is and realized how small I was. As tiny as I felt, I knew God could see me and must love me very much to have given me so much beauty to look upon. The train climbed higher and higher. I remember seeing a majestic bald eagle flying high above us. He flew with such style and freedom. My family and I watched as the wide winged creature with the hooked beak sailed in and out of the clouds like he was playing a game of hide and seek. How wonderful it would be to fly in the heavens and look down to the world below.

At last we reached the top of the mountain known as Pike's Peak. As we stepped out of the big red train and onto the platform of the rocky surface, I didn't know if it was the thin air or the breathtaking view that made my heart beat fast.

Drifts of fog began to cover us like soft white downy comforters, and the mist in the air made me think someone was spraying us with water.

I could see strong blue and green trees that looked as if they were made of velvet. Their branches reached out and up toward a blue sky that was now filled with layers of white and pastel colors. The colors created a twinkle and made it seem as if the trees were praising God.

Wildflowers surrounded reindeer that were feasting on red poppies. Birds of all species leisurely glided among the massive garden of trees. They looked as if they were waving hello as they dipped their lovely wings first to the left and then to the right.

In the west, the sun was just starting to settle when out of the blue heaven came a rainbow. Reaching from the north to the south, it filled the sky like a box of crayons had spilled out and melted into the firmament.

I was overwhelmed. Here I was, standing at the top of earth. I had never seen or felt such beauty before. My soul was filled with peace, and I could think only of heaven. And for just a moment, I actually thought we had arrived.

My name is Lynne and I'm a citizen of the eternal city.

It is a very big city, so big that no matter how many choose to live here, there is always room for one more.

This is my story.

God loved the world so much that He gave his one and only Son so that whoever believes in him may not be lost, but have eternal life.

John 3:16 NCV

The Way to the City

Behold I send an angel before thee, to keep thee in the way, and to bring thee into the place which I have prepared.

Exodus 23:20 KJV

It all seemed so strange. I was in a room I did not recognize, and there were so many people rushing everywhere. I could see my mother crying holding the hand of a girl who looked just like me. The girl seemed to be resting on a hard, cold table.

I tried to hug my mother and tell her not to cry. I couldn't understand. She didn't hear me or feel my hand as I touched her. I started to get nervous wondering what was happening. I was cold but not afraid. I looked around to find two shadows approaching me. I began feeling warmer as the two figures moved toward me. The room started changing. It was becoming softer and more colorful. I could see a yellow door that was turning pink. The longer I looked at it, the pinker it became. And then I felt someone pick me up and carry me though the unusual looking door.

Angel Adele and Angel Bella were smiling as they revealed themselves to me. Adele had a round face that never stopped smiling, and I could see a dimple on each of her chubby cheeks. Bella's face seemed to be a little more serious. They both wore long, white silk gowns with gold tassels hanging from rope-like belts. I was delighted to see them, although I had no idea where I was or what was happening.

Adele was the first to speak. "Take our hands, child, and we will take you to a place of complete happiness. It's called the City of God."

"City of God, do you mean heaven?" I asked.

A beam of light filled their faces with joy as they both answered, "Yes, that is exactly where we are going."

With no ground beneath us, we started on our way. With Adele holding my right hand and Bella holding on to my left, we seemed to be walking on solid air. It was as if they were carrying me. Bella directed our way to the staircase before us and said, "Lynne, this is the incredible stairway to heaven. At the end of their time on earth, God's people come up with the angels and enter the eternal kingdom by way of this staircase."

I watched as hundreds of angelic beings surrounded the glowing stairs that seemed to go on forever and ever. I felt enormous puffs of flowing white clouds feeding living nutrients into my spirit. The higher we went, the more aware I became of where I was going. Thousands and thousands of brilliant stars could be seen in the light.

When we reached the top of the stairs, I could see seven star lights. Each light had six points, and in the middle of each star light was a round, gold ball. Hanging from each point of every star light were little waterfalls of color that reminded me of the bubble lights on my grandfather's Christmas tree.

Bella smiled as she explained, "Lynne, these six pointed star-shaped lights symbolize God's rule over the universe in all six directions: north, south, east, west, up, and down. The gold ball in the middle of the star represents the spiritual dimension surrounded by the six universal directions. I know this is a lot to understand. So for now, just receive the joy that comes to you. Reach up your hand, Lynne, and touch them. They will become alive in your fingers."

I felt power filling my body, and I could hear the soft voice of angels repeating the words, "Welcome home."

Just as I reached up to touch the colors, my mouth and my ears started to tingle. Violet was the first color I became aware of. My mouth filled with the taste of sweet grapes, and immediately, violet spoke to me and told me of the meeting I was soon to have with my Savior. Indigo felt like a sponge, and the taste was smooth and spoke to me of my Savior's nobility. Blue tasted like candy gum drops and told me of God's eternal majesty. When I touched green, it made me feel as if I could fly, and the flavor of mint filled my mouth. Yellow felt and tasted very delicate as it took away any doubt I had. Orange created a juicy, fruity flavor that filled me with hope, and red was strong with the taste of cinnamon and told me of the promise of God's everlasting love and of the many blessings of heaven.

I loved the beauty of this amazing place. It made me feel like I was a princess in wonderland, but I could not understand how I got here.

"This is all so wonderful, Bella. But can I ask you and Adele a question? How did I get here?"

As Bella began to answer, she seemed to pull up a bench out of nowhere. "Of course you may ask us anything you like, but let's sit a while. Adele and I will do our best to answer your question."

The three of us sat down, and Adele pulled a bag

of cookies from her pocket. "Want one? They're chocolate, my favorite."

"Sure, chocolate's my favorite too."

"If you girls are ready, I would like to ask Lynne if she remembers what she was doing before we came for her."

"I remember that I just had a birthday, and … and school gave us a day off because of a man who discovered America."

"Was his name Christopher Columbus?" said Adele.

"Yeah, that's right. Do you know him?"

"Yes, I do. He lives in the town of Joppa."

Immediately, Bella interrupted. "Yes, he lives there with his son, Diego. We could take Lynne to see him sometime. For now, Adele, Lynne is telling us her story of what she remembers."

"Well, I remember I went with my aunt Jean and my cousins, David, Betty Jean, and Maralee Lou. We drove to Michigan on Sunday afternoon, and Sunday night we roasted marshmallows, sang songs, and laughed over silly jokes we made up."

"I know a joke."

"Not now, Adele! Let Lynne finish."

I was trying not to laugh at Adele, but she was so funny.

"When we woke up on Monday morning, Betty Jean and I could smell something delicious. It was the smell of pancakes."

"I love pancakes!" shouted Adele.

And then Bella looked Adele directly in the eyes and said, "Adele, please try not to interrupt."

Giggling, I started again. "Oh, the smell of pancakes and syrup filled the whole cottage. Maralee Lou and Aunt Jean had been busy cooking in the kitchen while Betty Jean and I had been sleeping upstairs in the loft over the garage. As Betty Jean and I were dressing for the day, I could hear David in the garage below. He was busy cleaning up inner tubes and getting things ready for a day at the beach."

"Bella, do you remember the time we had an assignment to help the little boy on the beach? I think it was in South America. I loved how the sand stuck between my toes." Then Adele looked down at her feet and said, "I don't think I ever did clean my toes!"

"Adele, please, Lynne is trying to tell us what happened."

"After we filled up on the yummy pancakes, we all helped Aunt Jean clean up the kitchen, and then we were off for a day of fun.

"We went to the garage to get our inner tubes, and David said he had cleaned the tubes but had found a few leaks and needed some time to fix them. He told me to ask Maralee Lou to take Betty Jean and me for a ride on the motorbike. He said he would probably be done by the time we got back."

"Hang on, please! Bella, can I just tell the story about the time I rode a motorbike?"

"I know that is a very funny story, Adele, but we can hear about your fun ride a little later. Go on, Lynne."

Adele was making me laugh again. I never thought of angels being so much fun.

"Betty Jean went first, and when she came back, the curls on her head were sticking out in all directions. She looked like she had a head of bouncing blond corkscrews!"

Now I had Adele laughing again as she yelled, "Wow, that must have been a fun ride!"

"I waited very patiently while Maralee took a

short break, and then it was my turn. We drove along Shoreline Road, and I loved the feeling of the wind blowing in my face as I turned my head to watch the big white waves. I began to realize just how beautiful God had made our world. Maralee stopped the bike so we could watch seagulls flying over the lake, and then she told me we would be taking a shortcut down the rocky road back to the cottage. She was sure the inner tubes would be ready. I loved the rocky road. It made me feel all jiggly inside. It was the best ride I ever had on a motorbike."

Bella reached down and took my hand as she asked me, "Lynne, what time was it when everyone went to the beach?"

"I'm not sure of the time, but it was right after we ate our picnic lunch. I remember how cold the water was on my feet, but the sun felt hot on my back and face. After we played in the tubes for a couple of hours, Betty Jean and I decided to make sand castles."

"If it's sand castles you would like to make, I'm sure Adele will be happy to make sand castles with you."

"I would love to make castles with you, Lynne. We have the most beautiful beaches in heaven. Ever since I got my toes filled with that wet sand, I can't stay away from anything wet or sandy!"

"When we were filling our buckets with sand, Betty Jean started laughing as she said, 'Lynne, your cheeks look like pink bubblegum.' And I said to her, 'And yours look just like red raspberries!'

"Maralee Lou looked at us both and said, 'You both look like beautiful rosebuds to me!' I think Maralee Lou loved us so much that even if we had mud on our faces she would have told us we looked like rosebuds.

Aunt Jean laughed at all of us as she yelled, 'All you beautiful rosebuds better get packing. It's been a long day, and it's time to head home.'"

Bella smiled as she said, "I'm sure Maralee Lou loves you and Betty Jean very much."

"Bella, I don't remember much more. When we got back to the cottage, we changed into our dry clothes, cleaned up the cottage, and put the inner tubes back in the garage. David carried the leftover groceries and our suitcases to the blue van. We started on our way back to Chicago, and the last thing I remember was feeling very sleepy when Maralee gave me a pillow and a soft blanket and a goodnight kiss. So tell me, why am I here with you and Adele?"

Bella was still holding my hand but just a little tighter when she said, "Lynne, I asked you about the time because you arrived here at seven o'clock. Before Adele and I tell you why you're here; I would like to tell you about a man called Mr. Samuel. Mr. Samuel was a big man. He weighed two hundred and fifty pounds and stood six feet three inches. He was always cheerful, and you could usually find him whistling a happy tune. He had a job driving a big semi-truck and usually drove from one city to another. Mr. Samuel was delivering a load of furniture to a warehouse in Michigan.

"Bella, don't forget that he has a wife, Sophie, and two young boys, Theodore and Jackson."

"Let me finish, Adele. He began to feel a pain in his left arm. As the pain became worse, he decided he should pull off to the side of the road, but then another pain came and another. The pains were so sharp that he lost control of the truck. It was seven o'clock when the truck jolted to the center of the highway, and Mr.

Samuel felt helpless as he saw a dark blue van filled with people coming toward him. Knowing that his truck was about to hit the van, he tried desperately to stop the truck, but he hurt so badly he could hardly even hold on to the steering wheel. At that moment, all Mr. Samuel could do was pray for his family and the people in the van. Praying was the last thing Mr. Samuel remembered. Lynne, you told me and Adele your Aunt Jean's van was blue."

"Yes, Bella, it was navy blue. Wait! Are you telling me it was Aunt Jean's van that Mr. Samuel's truck hit?"

"Yes, Lynne, that's what we are telling you."

I looked up at Adele as she took my other hand in hers and said, "Lynne, your life, as well as the lives of your aunt, your cousins, and Mr. Samuel, changed forever the moment Mr. Samuel lost control of his truck. We are here to bring you to Jesus. God has given you a new body and a new mind, and you will live with him forever and ever. God has a special plan for you."

"Can Mama and Daddy, Joe and Kevin, and Carol Ann and Jeanne come with me too?"

"No, Lynne, the rest of your family must wait until Jesus calls for them. Believe me, it won't feel like very long before all of your family will be here with you. If you like, Adele and I will be glad to teach you how to peek down at earth. You will be able to see your mom and the rest of your family while you are waiting for them. Your aunt and Betty Jean are here waiting for you now."

"How soon can you teach me to peek down at earth?"

"Be patient, child, for it is not yet time. Let's continue on our journey."

I was losing all sense of time and not sure how I felt about all this. I thought about Mr. Samuel and hoped he was not sad.

Just as I was about to ask where we were going, Bella said, "We will be at the east side of heaven's wall, in a moment." And then I saw a twelve-story wall. It was separated by three sets of gates. Each gate was made from a single brilliant white pearl. Adele told me there were also three sets of gates on the north, south, and the west side. Every level of the wall had a name written on it: John, Peter, James…

"Bella, the names on the wall, are they the names of the twelve apostles?"

"Yes, Lynne, they are the names of the twelve apostles of Jesus."

"A couple of weeks ago at Sunday school, my teacher, Miss Goldie, told us about the twelve men that followed Jesus when he was on earth."

"I'm glad you went to Sunday school, Lynne. Did Miss Goldie tell you about heaven?"

"She told me that heaven was made of beautiful jewels. She said it was the most beautiful place in the universe. And the best part was I could see Jesus anytime I wanted."

"Well, she was right. This is the most beautiful place, and in just a minute you will be in the arms of Jesus."

"Lynne, look, the name of Matthias is written on the first level of the wall."

"Yes, Adele, and the color of the wall is a dark red. What's the name of that precious stone?"

"That gem is called jasper. The next level is made of sapphire, and Simon the Zealot is written on this beautiful blue stone. A halo of orange with Phillip's name is written across the chalcedony layer. The name of James is engraved in emerald green. If you look up you can see the middle of the wall has a ring of brown and white marble with the name James the Younger written on it. Above this polished stone is a wide metallic string that is actually a light curve setting off bursts of energy. John is next on the red level, called sardius. Seventh is chrysolyte with the name Bartholomew. Thomas is written on pink beryl, and the yellow topaz has Andrew's name written on it. The tenth layer is green chrysoprasus and has the name Matthew. The next level of the wall is made of clear red quartz with the name of Thaddaeus written on a layer of jacinth.

"Lynne, do you like the color amethyst on the top level of the wall?"

"Oh yes, Adele, purple is my favorite color. It reminds me of my favorite purple dress, the one Mama bought me for my birthday. And I see the name of my favorite apostle is on the purple level."

"That's my favorite too! I love Peter!"

I was laughing because Bella was shaking her head as she said, "Adele, I think everything is your favorite."

Bella told me the foundation represented people. Each person was very different and every person very essential to the kingdom. I wasn't sure what that meant, but I was sure Bella knew what she was talking about.

I asked Adele, "How do you know which gate to use?"

"That's easy; each gate has a purpose, and you will learn later why there are three sets of gates on each side of the wall. The gate we will be using today is the middle gate at the east entrance, which is called the welcome gate. Everyone entering heaven must enter through this gate. It's my favorite gate because I love to see how happy it makes everyone the moment they enter. Sometimes the apostle Peter waits on the other side to welcome people. He likes to know what's going on, and he certainly doesn't miss much!"

As we stepped through the east gate, I could see a threshold. It was made of a golden metal, and I could feel love coming from it. Bella said, "The threshold looks like a twinkling star when Jesus steps over holding a child in his arms. Lynne, when you were on earth, you actually saw this miracle happen. What you assumed was a brilliant star flickering in the sky was actually God taking one of his children into his kingdom."

I began to take a step forward when Bella stopped me. "We must wait for just a moment. Jesus," Bella said, "will carry you over."

Then it happened. My God appeared, and I heard him say, "Come unto me," as he gently lifted me up into his loving arms. Never before had I felt so safe and peaceful and so loved as that moment in the arms of Jesus, my Savior.

As we started over the threshold, I could see him through my own reflection in the mirror-like pearl gates. When Jesus set me upon this kingdom of his, I knew he and I had a new kind of connection. I could not only feel his presence, but I could also see him face-to-face, anytime and anywhere, here in his home of glory.

Greetings and Angels

After this I heard what sounded like the roar of a
great multitude in heaven, hallelujah, salvation, and
glory, and power belong to our God.

Revelations 19:1 NIV

I was so happy to be with Jesus that I hadn't noticed
my grandmother and the others. They were all waiting for me: grandparents, great-grandparents, aunts,
uncles, and cousins. There were others there too, people I had not known while living on earth.

I turned as I felt a hand on my shoulder. "Great-
grandma, is that really you? I'm so happy to see you."
She was hugging me so tight I could hardly talk.
"Grandma, I missed you. I'm so happy you're here. Is
great-grandpa here too?"

"Yes, he will be with us shortly, and he has something for you."

I noticed children of all ages coming toward me.
One little girl looked to be about five years old. She
had dark braided hair and big, round, dark eyes, and
she was running so fast that I thought she might fall.
And then Grandma said, "Lynne, I would like to
introduce you to your cousin Charlotte."

I whispered to Great-grandma, "How come I don't
remember her?"

"Charlotte is one of the chosen who came to be
with us before she was conceived on earth."

"How come she is not a baby then?"

"Because in heaven, the chosen are any age their parents want them to be."

Charlotte began shouting. "Look, look, everyone. Lynne is here." We were laughing, and Charlotte started jumping up and down and hugging me.

I noticed the children were carrying beautiful flowers with tiny silver bells between them. The bells made a tingling sound that reminded me of the little bells Miss Goldie gave us to ring on Easter Sunday.

"Grandma, do you think I could have some of those beautiful flowers with the bells?"

And then I heard a familiar voice.

"Welcome home, Lynne." Grandpa Joe laughed, and then he handed me the biggest bunch of purple violets I had ever seen. And in the middle of each flower was a little silver bell. The flowers smelled like the perfume on Mama's dresser.

"Thank you so much, Grandpa. They're beautiful, and I love the bells! Grandpa Joe, have you seen my nana?"

"Yes, your nana is here, and you will see her soon. But now you should meet with your guardian angel, Cara."

I could hear thousands of angelic beings singing praises to the Lord and welcoming my arrival into the city when Cara presented herself to me. "Hello, Lynne, my name is Cara. I'm your guardian angel, and I'm very happy to meet you. What a nice purse you are wearing on your shoulder."

I wasn't quite sure what all this was about but knew I was where I belonged.

"I'm happy to meet you, Cara. I'm glad you like my purse. Mama gave it to me for my birthday. I know I had a guardian angel on earth, but I could never see you. How come I can see and hear you now?"

"Lynne, on earth you only had five senses. Now God has given you another sense. It's called heart sense. Heart sense gives strength and nourishes your other five senses. What that means, Lynne, is that now you will be able to understand and see things that were not possible on earth. It is my job to teach you about your heart sense."

From that first meeting with Cara, I could tell I was going to like her a lot, and she would be my special angel forever. As we sat talking on a beautiful gold bench, I noticed Jesus watching us. He had a big smile on his face, and I could feel his emotions from the top of my head to the bottom of my feet. My Savior was happy to have me home. And I was happy to be home too!

As I was listening to Cara, I noticed the other angels. They were so enchanting as they moved about with strength and grace. "Lynne, everyone here has different responsibilities and tasks to complete. Angel Eldon gives out new assignments each season. Eldon is in charge of all orders. You will be meeting him soon, and I know you will like him. He is really very nice, but he takes his work so seriously that he sometimes seems a little intimidating."

"That's okay. I'm sure he does a good job, and that probably makes Jesus very happy."

"Yes, Jesus is always happy when we do well. Lynne, I'm here to help you with your assignments, and I will always be close by if you want or need me. Some angels are storytellers, others are recorders of facts, and some are here to worship and praise God continually. Archangels Michael and Gabriel stay very busy. They travel to earth several times each new season bringing the good news."

"Do you think I could meet Michael and Gabriel? Miss Goldie read us stories about them. I think Gabriel was the one who told Jesus' mother that she would have a baby, and Michael was the chief commander of the army of God."

"Yes, that is right. Miss Goldie was a very good teacher. Gabriel and Michael are on assignment now, but when they get back, I'm sure they will want to meet you."

"It must be great to fly to earth and back all the time."

"Actually, Lynne, I like staying here. I'm not fond of heights. Although I do like to fly sometimes!"

"Cara, tell me about those angels that fly so fast. When I was with Adele and Bella, I thought I saw something fly by me, but they went so fast I wasn't sure if I was imagining something. They looked like they had eyes everywhere."

"No, that was not your imagination, Lynne. Cherubim and seraphim angels are the guardians of the heavens. They fly so fast it looks like a blur as they hurry to do the work God has assigned them. Seraphim can start fires with the tip of their fingers and even hold hot coals in their hands. They have eyes in the front and back of their heads so they can see in all directions."

"Why does God want them to see everything at once?"

"They're called the watchers. Eldon told me they must watch the stars and planets every second. If one small star would spiral out of place, the whole universe would collide. The galaxy has billions of stars. If a planet or star should start to fall, the watchers are fast enough to grab it and put it back again. Sometimes a star will lose its shine, and if that happens, one of the seraphim watchers can go light it up again with his fingertip."

"I thought they looked so weird, even a little creepy. But I'm sure glad God is so smart. It would be terrible if the universe fell apart. Now when I see them I will think how beautiful they really are."

"It may seem strange when you see someone who looks different or creepy, but you are learning fast. We should not judge someone by the way they look but look at them and see the good they do for God and his universe."

As Cara was talking, another angel came up to us. He was quite tall and wore a funny blue hat with a white bird perched on top. He was dressed in a white shirt with big blue buttons in the shape of birds, and his blue and white striped pants glowed like they were made from metal. In spite of his appearance, the deep sound of his voice startled me. "Hello, Cara; hello, Lynne. Lynne, has Cara been telling you about assignments?"

"Hello, are you Eldon?"

"Lynne just arrived, Eldon. Does she need her assignment given to her so soon?"

"Yes, Cara, I'm very busy, and I want to make sure I don't miss anyone. We have many new arrivals this season."

"Very well, what is her assignment?"

"Lynne, your first assignment is to write a story. I want you to record everything you see and experience. That includes people and angels that you meet along your way. Take notes; write how you feel as you learn and enjoy your adventures. When you finish, I will take your journal to Gabriel, and he will communicate your story to the people on earth. I know this sounds like a big assignment, but your story will bring encouragement to many."

"I will do my best, Eldon."

"That's all I ask," he said as he handed me the most extraordinary journal. I wondered if he knew how much I enjoyed writing. Mama had bought me a small diary once, and I wrote in it every day. The journal was in the shape of an unusual door. It reminded me of a door that was in a story I once read. A princess wanted to go to a castle in the sky. To get there she had to go through a beautiful old door that had a window in it. She thought she had a problem because the door didn't have a handle on it. She had to find the secret that opened the door. The poor girl never did find the secret and never got to the castle in the sky. What she didn't realize was all she had to do was knock and the door would open.

The outer edge of my journal was made of gold. The center had an open window, and I could see a white dove flying over a rainbow of colors. There seemed to be an invisible light coming from within the book. And when I opened it, I was surprised to find that the pages were made of a shiny silver cloth. "Cara, look at the pages in my journal. Will I be able to write on them? I always wrote on paper."

"Only if you have this wonderful pencil," she said as she offered me a long, shiny stick. "If you look closely at your journal, you will notice a small opening on its side. This is where you should keep the special silver pencil. I can see now that you're feeling a bit overwhelmed, but remember, Lynne, I'm here to help you. If there is anything you need, you can count on me."

"Cara, I'm so glad you're my special angel."

"Lynne, did you know that here in heaven if you have a desire to learn something you will learn it and never forget it?"

"That's amazing; you make it sound so simple."

"It is simple, because God wants you to be happy, and he knows that if you know more about him you will love him even more. Remember when you were in school and the teacher would tell you to look something up in the dictionary? I have a book something like that."

"Yeah, I remember. My mom had a big red one on her desk at home, and she always had me look up words I could not spell. She told me if I looked up the word myself then I would remember much better than if she told me how to spell it."

"Well, my book is red too. It's called *God's Reference Book.* I'll show you."

Without saying another word, Cara reached down and took a big red book from somewhere. I'm not sure if it was under her robe or under the bench we were sitting on, but there it was, the most beautiful book I had ever seen. The outside was embellished with yellow-green stones. These stones sent out rays of light onto large gold bands of ribbon, which turned the pages to reveal the written words.

"Lynne, unlike most reference books, God lists his words in order of importance. Look at the first word in the book. It is the word *grace*. Read what it says next to the word."

"*The love of God fulfilled. The finished work of Jesus Christ. Our father and his only begotten Son, Jesus Christ, give grace freely; therefore, all who wish may enter heaven and live eternally in the presence of true love.*"

"Look at the picture under the definition. God is showing us, not just telling us, that he and his Son welcome every person with loving arms."

"Cara, that is the most beautiful picture I have ever seen. The colors look like they are alive."

"Later on we will study other words and meanings in this wonderful book, and we will talk more of your first assignment. But now I want to finish telling you about the other angels."

And just like that, Cara put the big red book back from where it came.

"If you enjoy music, Lynne, you will love the choir angels and the school of musicology."

"I love music and singing and dancing. Mama took me to dance lessons when I lived with her. And I always wanted to play the piano. My nana loves to dance and sing. I haven't seen Nana yet, but I know she is here."

"Yes, your nana is here, and you will see her when we're done here."

"Thanks, Cara. I'm really anxious to see her, and I know she is eager to see me."

"There is a multitude of angels called living creatures. These creatures have extraordinary voices and sing with infinite beauty. Sopranos, baritones, and tenor voices fill the air with colorful and spectacular animation. Like moving pictures, their voices create expressions of God's eternal love. A gentle wind carries the fragrance of water rising into the atmosphere, and a delicate light is released as their voices beam into the heavens giving an aura of romance and peace. When angels sing, their voices carry vibrations that produce echoes. The repetition of sound creates a powerful aura that causes sparkling butterflies to glide through the sky.

"Singers are joined by other groups of living creatures playing instruments of all shapes and sizes. Varieties of instruments produce musical tones and sounds of different chords. With great flexibility and strength, the living creatures make up an orchestra of heavenly organized sounds. As the angels perform, each individual musical note blends with the others, and together the incredible connection travels throughout heaven. The connection causes a chemical change that induces brilliant colors and shapes that form hundreds of multicolored stars. Angels set off energy so powerful the music and voices of the angels can be heard and seen from every section of heaven. Sometimes, if the people on earth listen carefully, they might be able to hear the sounds and enjoy this musical ensemble as well."

"Do you think my mom and family have ever heard the music? My cousin Ben has probably heard it. He can hear each individual sound of every instrument in the orchestra. He has great ears. When can I sign up at the school for music lessons?"

"Not now, there is much to do today. But I will speak to Ariel. She is in charge of the school, and I know a man named Franz. He is very talented, and I know he could teach you how to play the piano. He also has an instrument called the celesta. It is similar to a piano but smaller and has a softer tone. I think you will like it. Lynne, I know you're anxious to see Nana, but I think you should start your journal. You can write what you have seen and experienced since you have arrived. I'm sure Nana will be glad to know that you have already received your first assignment and have started so soon."

"That sounds like a good idea, Cara. I'll give it a try." As I wrote the words, *It all seemed so strange.* I couldn't believe my eyes; the silver cloth began changing from silver to yellow. "Cara, look, the cloth is changing its color."

And then as I began writing about angels, I felt my eyes and ears were playing tricks on me because now the pages became a beautiful pure white and I could hear Bella's voice in my spirit. She was telling me the meaning of the names of angels.

Adele—cheerful

Bella—beautiful

Cara—beloved friend

Eldon—persuasive

Gabriel—bearer of truth, joy, and love

Michael—chief prince

Elizabeth—watchful

Elnora—luminous

Flora—flower

Gevariah—strong and forceful

Cherubim angels—guardians of heaven

Seraphim angels—radiate pure light

Living creatures—animated musical beings

"Cara, as the pages turned from yellow to white, I could hear Bella speaking to me in my heart."

"Yes, I know. Isn't it wonderful? And it looks as if your journal will fit perfectly in your lovely purse. If you're ready, we can see your Nana now."

"Oh yes, thank you."

I was so surprised as Cara took me by the hand and we started flying. I thought any minute I would sprout wings, but it never happened. We just sailed smoothly through the air like we were on a glider. We landed directly in front of an unusual looking park. Nothing was the color it was supposed to be. The grass was blue, the sky green, and the trees and plants were different shades of red and purple. Several families and angels were waving hello as we landed, and everyone was carrying a picnic basket. "Cara, where are we?"

"This is a park we come to when we want to be silly. Your nana told me she would meet us here."

"Yoo-hoo, Lynne, it's me, Adele. Isn't this the greatest park you've ever seen? Want to join me for a picnic lunch?"

"Hi, Adele. No thanks, maybe next time. I'm waiting for Nana."

And then I spotted her. She was running toward us. "Nana, Nana," I shouted as I jumped into her arms and kissed her. "I love you; I love you." Nana had crossed the threshold into heaven when I was only six earth years old, and I didn't realize how much I had missed her. She looked the same but somehow different. Her dark brown hair and green eyes were the same color, but now her hair was shinier, like someone had put oil on it, and she wasn't wearing her eyeglasses. "Nana, where are your glasses?"

"Isn't it wonderful, Lynne? I don't need them anymore. When I arrived here, God gave me new eyes. The same color as the old ones, but these work better and will last for eternity."

"And he gave you shiny hair too!"

"Yes, he did, and now I want to take you someplace special."

"Nana, I want to show you my new journal. Eldon gave it to me. It's for my first assignment."

"What a lovely book. I like the light coming from it."

"Nana, I have never seen a journal like this. It's so amazing; when I wrote with this special silver pencil, the silver pages turned yellow, and when I began writing about the angels, the pages turned pure white."

"That is amazing. I'm glad you are having so much fun."

My New Home

In my Father's house are many mansions; if it were not so, I would have told you. I go to prepare a place for you.

John 14:2 KJV

I was excited that Nana had something special to show me. "Where are we going? What kind of surprise do you have for me?" But Nana wouldn't tell. She just smiled and said, "If I told you, then it wouldn't be a surprise, would it?" I knew wherever we were going was going to be wonderful.

From the moment we started walking, I became aware of the lush blue carpet of grass and brilliant flowers under our feet. The grass and flowers didn't flatten as we walked but sprang up immediately as if we had never stepped on them. Majestic red and purple trees along the way had bluebirds sitting on strong nimble branches that seemed to bend to a tune the birds were singing. I could hear music flowing from a current of air that encircled the trees. It was so exciting. Nana and I started singing along with the birds. It was a tune I had never heard before, and yet I knew every word. With carefree hearts, we were singing praises to our Father in perfect harmony. The air was pure with a slight scent of perfume, and the atmosphere gave me a new strength and energy I had never experienced. I knew I could run, and jump, and have great fun without ever tiring.

I noticed a silver pathway at the edge of the grass curving away from the direction we were headed. The silver trail was lined with red trees reaching upward hundreds of feet. A smooth oval canopy at the top of each tree was filled with a maze of leaves and branches that was home to parrots, hornbills, big-eared bats, and blue and orange tree frogs. Nana told me there were many more animals I could not see from where we were standing, and one day soon she would take me down the silver path that led to a wonderful place. "What kind of place?" I asked her.

"It is called the city of Lianas," she answered, "because of the special vines that grow on the tall trees. The entire city is overflowing with exotic flowers and animals, and the citizens who live there make unusual food from the plants and flowers. They also like to cook with chocolate, cinnamon, and honey."

"Let's go soon, please, Nana."

"We sure will," she said, smiling. "But first things first."

We walked through many towns and cities that surrounded the main city of heaven, and then Nana asked, "Lynne, would you like to have your very own place?"

"I think having my own place to live would be fun. But I would want you to be close by. Do the people here always stay with their families? If Mama and Dad were here, I would want them to live near us too. Maybe we could all live in houses that connect to one other."

"It's funny you should say that, Lynne, because there are many families that do live in connecting houses. Every place here was designed especially for the person or the family that will live in it. God made everyone different. And he made every house different. He knew what would make every person and family happy, and he planned ahead for everyone. Lynne, look at the many colors of the unusual homes. They are much more powerful than the colors on earth, and like a big kaleidoscope, they come together until they overlap and burst into a carnival of brilliance. And did you know, Lynne, that each color has a special meaning? There are many shades and tones of every color, but the basic color of each is similar to those you have seen before. Here is a list for your journal."

Color	Meaning
Yellow	Hope
Purple	Happiness
Green	Unity
White	Pure
Pink	Compassion
Brown	Comfort
Orange	Peace
Red	Love
Blue	Royalty
Gold	Eternal
Silver	Redemption

"Nana, I never knew colors had meanings. Now I know why my favorite dress makes me happy. Because it's purple! Where do all of these colors come from, Nana?"

"All of the colors came from a dye made from shellfish. Select groups of men create the dye from snails and cuttlefish and other aquatic shellfish that exist only here in heaven. In the main city, along the river's edge, is a great building made of stone. It is set deep in the ground close to the shore of the river and has rooms built of glass with river water flowing through the middle. The rooms hold all of the sea creatures the men use to make the special dyes.

"The men extract clear liquid from the glands of the shellfish and then put it into several different stone bowls. The bowls are then placed in areas of special lighting. Ultraviolet rays change the clear color to several different shades and tones of red, yellow, and blue. By timing the ultraviolet rays precisely, a new color can be achieved by using one or all of the basic three colors."

"What do they do with the colors once they make them?"

"They give the brilliant colors to others. People use them to dye cloth and for painting."

"Can we go there sometime? I would love to watch the men as they make new colors."

"Sure, I'll be glad to take you."

Nana and I arrived in the city of Isaiah at 7 Romans Road, directly across from Proverbs Avenue. I could not believe my eyes. It was the most enchanting cottage I had ever seen. With a big smile on her face, Nana looked at me and said, "Lynne, this is the house that Jesus prepared especially for you."

The only thing I could say was, "Wow!"

It was designed like those houses you would see in a fairy-tale book. The entrance, with its side-by-side doors, was the color of buttermilk. Showy multi-colored butterflies constantly flew around the frame of the doors that always remained partly open so anyone passing by could enter if they wished to visit for a while. As I stepped inside, the first thing I noticed was the awesome ceiling. It was crystal clear, made so I could look up and see the bells of heaven. They were ruby red and shaped like trumpets and had large silver candles hanging from the inside of them. Like a giant hand reaching down, the wind blew gently, causing the candles to strike against the bells. This made the bells shine brightly, and a cheerful musical sound filled the air immediately in celebration of God.

Because of the see-through ceiling and the wide doorways, the rooms seemed to flow together as one. My favorite room was the library. I remembered asking Mama why we couldn't have a library at our house, and she had said only rich people have libraries in their homes. I guess I'm a rich person now. This was the biggest room in the house. The floor was made of a special glass that didn't break when I walked on it. Under the glass were rare antique manuscripts with encouraging words written by wise scholars that lit up when I walked across the floor. I especially liked the verse written by a wise man by the name of David. He wrote, "Surely goodness and mercy will follow me all the days of my life, and I will dwell in the house of the Lord forever."

The walls of the library were covered with my favorite colors, purple and blue. The wooden walls looked like silk, and painted on the walls were pictures of happy children singing and dancing in beautiful costumes. Shiny wooden shelves lined the sidewalls and held books on every subject.

I was looking over the books when I noticed a wide shelf at the bottom of the bookcase. Several cookbooks sat alongside a large square oven. I couldn't believe my eyes. My first thought was that somehow Mama must have known this was here waiting for me. Just four days before I arrived here, I had a birthday. Mama and I had planned to go to the toy store after my holiday in Michigan. We were going to buy an Easy Bake Oven. Then I met Adele and Bella and things changed. Now, here it was on the bottom shelf. The most magnificent purple and white Easy Bake Oven anyone had ever seen. Once again I was speechless, and the only word I could utter was, "Wow!"

There was a big, comfy, overstuffed chair sitting directly in front of an orange and brown fireplace. A carved mantelpiece made from red cedar surrounded the fireplace and was inscribed with the words, "Teach me thy ways, Lord." Inside the fireplace, red and yellow flames leaped through speckled logs that gave off a feeling of warmth but somehow never burned hot. Nana told me to clap my hands and the fire would change colors, and if I clapped my hands twice, the fire would disappear. I would have to clap my hands again for it to reappear. I started clapping my hands to turn the fire off and on and change its colors when Nana said, "Lynne, I have a great idea. Why don't you sit in the comfy chair and catch up on your writing. I will make some of my delicious chocolate cookies."

"That sounds wonderful, Nana. I haven't had any of your tasty chocolate cookies since I was five years old!"

Just as I was finishing writing on the lovely purple pages, I looked, and she was coming back into the room with a tray of warm cookies and ice-cold milk. We sat and talked some more as we enjoyed the incredible, scrumptious cookies.

Opposite the fireplace was a large window in the shape of an octagon, and from it, I could see a garden. As I moved closer to the window, I could see someone in the distance. She seemed familiar. My curiosity was growing as I stepped out of the back door that was next to the window to get a better view. The girl had started running toward me. Still, I could not make out whom she was. Her hair was light and her eyes were shinning. And then I recognized her amazing smile. Now I was running toward her as I heard her call out my name. "Lynne, Lynne!"

By the time we reached one another, we both had tears of happiness running down our cheeks. The last time I had seen Betty Jean was when we were in the van with Maralee Lou, Aunt Jean, and Dave. We were heading home from Michigan when both of us had fallen asleep, and now, here we were together, in a place of wonder and beauty.

"Isn't this place as beautiful as any place can be?" she said. We were jumping with joy and turning around and around until we were dizzy with gladness.

"Yes, it is," I replied. "It is even more beautiful than Pike's Peak in the summer.

"And our houses are joined together by this garden God created especially for us," said Betty Jean, "and we will be together forever and ever. Everything is just perfect!"

"Nana, look, Betty Jean is here!"

"Yes, I know, Lynne, and she will always be with us. Look, girls, there is a special garden Jesus prepared just for the two of you. He has also given you both a beautiful lake to share and some very special animals to call your very own. Shall we go check it out?"

As she started running, Betty Jean yelled out, "Come on, Lynne, I'll race you!"

"Can't beat me. I'm fast."

For a while we just stood staring at the garden. This couldn't be real. It was better than I could have ever imagined. I was staring at the adorable little capuchin monkeys swinging high between the banana and cacao trees when I heard Betty Jean. "Have you ever even dreamed of something like this?"

There were large pink and purple bushes that looked like giant feathers. They bordered a see-through railing made of blue diamonds that had a wide swinging gate separating Betty Jean's place from mine. Weeds in our garden were actually flowers that shot up tall and wild in shades of orange and purple. The soil was not soil as it was on earth. Here the soil was made of gold dust. Nana said if we placed a red seed in this special soil, the seed would grow into a red flower. If we planted a blue seed, the flower would grow blue. We had hundreds of different colored seeds. Betty Jean and I laughed when we discovered a new color. We starting blowing into the gold dust, and it began flying all over the yard. Nana said it made the grass look like a big present that someone had wrapped for a party.

"Lynne, look over there," yelled Betty Jean. "Llamas with long graceful necks and big round eyes are walking through the roses, and the roses don't even mind. I can see a meadow filled with alfalfa hay. That must be what they eat when they get hungry."

"Girls, look over there. Can you see the gentle black bears walking through the blackberry bushes?"

"Yes, Nana," I said, "and there are white-tailed deer drinking from the waterfall."

Of all the animals we found in our garden, Betty Jean's favorite was a little, fluffy, white lamb. She picked him up in her arms and looked at his sweet face and said, "Hello Babe, you have the bluest eyes and the longest black curly eyelashes I have ever seen."

And then the strangest thing happened. Babe looked at Betty Jean and said, "Yes, I am rather cute."

Betty Jean was so shocked that she actually dropped Babe on the grass. "Lynne, did you hear that?"

"What, you never heard an animal talk before?" Babe laughed.

Betty Jean and I were not sure if we should laugh or answer the lamb.

"Girls, God made the animals to communicate with us. Remember, you are not on earth anymore. In heaven everything and everyone is the way that God planned them to be. Even the animals."

I was laughing and thought to myself, *I can't wait to write about this in my journal!*

Betty picked up Babe and said, "Yes, you are rather cute, and I am sorry I dropped you."

"That's all right," answered Babe. "The grass is soft."

I felt two kittens rubbing against my leg. I bent down to pet them. One was a calico, and the other was pure white with a small red mark shaped like a heart on her forehead. As I started walking, they both began to follow me. I started running, and the faster I ran the faster they ran. The kittens and I were playing this silly game when we noticed a beautiful sheep dog watching us. I stopped running to get a better look at this big beautiful dog.

It was as if he could read my mind because I was thinking how much I would like to have him for my very own. He was looking at me with eager, almond-shaped dark eyes. His sable and white coat made him look incredibly dignified.

I was so taken with him I didn't hear Nana as she came up to me. "Lynne, I think that dog is here for you."

"Really, you think he belongs to me?"

"Yes, honey, I'm sure he does!"

"I think I'll call him Micah." As soon as I said Micah, he came running to me, and I knew he would be my dog forever.

Micah and I were getting acquainted when the most extraordinary horse came up to us and introduced himself. "Hello," he said. "My name is Noble."

Noble was a beautiful white stallion that stood sixteen hands high. His mane and tail were the color of taffy, and he had big round eyes the color of dark chocolate with thick eyelashes that looked like miniature feathered fans when he blinked.

"I'm thrilled to make your acquaintance," I said, laughing. "Have you met my dog, Micah?"

"Yes, Micah and I arrived here on the same day. When we were on earth, we were not part of a family, so both Micah and I are pleased to belong to your family. I'm really quite nice and very gentle for my size, and I would be so pleased to be your friend."

"And I'm here to tell you we will both be here for you whenever you need us," explained Micah.

I gave them both a big hug, and together we laughed as I told them both, "I love you."

"Well, that's settled then. Would you like to go for a ride? I can sit down and you could climb on my back. I promise I will stand up gently so you won't fall."

As I gave him a kiss on his soft silky muzzle, I asked him if he could wait a while. "I want to see the rest of my garden and then talk with Nana a little more."

"Sure, I'll be here waiting with Micah whenever you are ready," he answered.

Nana and Betty Jean were walking toward me when I heard Betty Jean call my name. "Lynne, let's go see the lake." As I turned around, I saw the kittens following me. I smiled as I said, "I will call you Goodness and Mercy because you both seem to follow me wherever I go!"

Nana smiled as she said, "I think those names will be perfect."

Butterflies and honeybees flew around purple violets and jasmine that grew along a pathway of gold leading to Lake Glorious. The water was so clear I could see two dolphins swimming above the white sand at the bottom of this heart-shaped pool. Delfy, the larger of the two dolphins, had a beak-like snout and was light gray. She was also the more curious of the two. Dafney had a long gray patch on her foreside leading to a short, dark gray beak. She liked to show off, jumping high and then plunging into the water while making silly noises. They both loved to play ball, but I think their favorite time, as well as mine, was when Betty Jean and I tossed rings to them so they could catch the metal circles on their noses.

On our way back to my house, Betty Jean said her mom wanted Nana and I to come for a visit. "I would like very much to see Aunt Jean. Do you and your mom live in the same house?" I asked. "Or do your houses connect?"

"Yes, Mom and I wanted to live together. Mom said time goes so quickly it won't take long before David and Maralee and my brother, Dan, will be here with us, and she would like it if we all lived together."

"You know, girls, time here is different than on earth. Did you notice we do not have calendars or clocks? God decides when a day will end and when another will begin."

"I'm not sure I understand, Nana, but I know now how much God wants us to be happy."

"In God's kingdom, a day in heaven can be as long or short as God speaks it. The beginning of a new day has a different color than the closing of the day. The onset of day is the color of energy, pure white, and the day concludes with restful amber filling the land and sky. Every so often a gentle mist falls in the early hours of the day. It will feel silky-smooth on your skin. At the end of a day, God sometimes surprises us with drops of rain that look like crushed diamonds. If you happen to catch one in your hand, it softens and becomes delicious custard."

I asked Nana, "Can the people eat the custard?"

"Oh yes, it's the best you have ever tasted! The children like to watch the older citizens lick this sugary vanilla from their hands and fingers. It's really very funny because the custard melts away if not eaten quickly!"

Betty Jean and I were laughing as she said, "That must be hilarious. Next time it rains, let's go watch the old folks."

"I can hardly wait for the rain to come!"

"Girls, Jesus knows how to keep us carefree and

happy until that day when we will all be together again with our loved ones. And when that day comes, if it's possible, we will enjoy ourselves even more."

As I wrote about a secret doorway connecting my library to Nana's, I wanted to be sure not to miss anything in Nana's house. As I began, the pages now became a soft blue. Nana's home was very elegant. Wide steps made of white granite led up to the front of Nana's house, which had five columns that separated the windows. The windows were actually glass roses framed in solid gold lace. The double-door entrance had glasswork fashioned to look like beautiful birds and led to the reception area where a long gold table stood on a white marbled floor. On top of the table were several rosy-colored baskets. The baskets were kept filled with a hodgepodge of candies for all of the children that came to visit. Inside, the main room was decorated with chestnut-colored wooden furniture covered with soft white and blue linen. Sky-blue velvet walls were covered with soft white angel hair positioned in a special way so it looked as if the walls were floating. A golden staircase with steps covered in royal blue carpet was positioned in the center of the living room. At the top of the stairs, an indoor garden had elegant plants and flowers of every color that sat in big white china pots on a diamond-filled stone floor.

The indoor garden extended out to a balcony overlooking the courtyard, which was filled with roses of red and white. There were big gold chairs shaped to look like angel wings with embroidered silk cushions. These beautiful chairs were placed next to bright green bushes that overflowed with delicious fruit. Nana and I sat here and read stories of the saints that lived on earth long before us.

She said one day soon we would visit with those we had read about. I could hardly wait to visit with Francis of Assisi. He lived in a garden with his animal friends. I wanted to talk with the mother of Jesus and a boy named David who liked to sing and dance for the Lord. Suddenly, I could hear the soft sound of a trumpet, and a sweet fragrance filled the air. "Nana, why is someone playing a trumpet, and what is that I smell?"

"That means it's God's seventh hour, Lynne. In the middle of each day, at the seventh hour, the air we breathe becomes filled with the awareness and fragrance of God. Can you hear the soft musical sounds? Those are the bells of heaven, and that sweet odor you are smelling is the odor of God spilling into the heavens. This is when the citizens of heaven prepare to gather at the throne room. If there is anything special you wish to present to God, this is the time. It can be an affection of love or something you had accomplished in his name. It can be something you have made especially for him. Whatever your gift might be, it will always be received joyfully."

The Throne Room

… Being with you will fill me with joy; at your right
hand I will find pleasure forever.

Psalm 16:11 NCV

Before we left for the throne room, we prepared ourselves by cleaning our hands and feet with soap that
had a scent of honey. Then we dressed ourselves in our
finest garments of white. My white silk dress looked
like a wedding dress. It had long wide sleeves and a
belt made from pure white gardenia pedals. My dress
was so long that it touched the top of my white linen
sandals.

"Nana, should we walk to the throne room? And can
I bring my journal?"

"Lynne, the throne room is a very holy place. This
is a time of holy worship, and God wants your full
attention while you worship him. Open your journal
now and write the words *throne room* and you will see
what I'm talking about."

As soon as I finished the *e* in the word *throne,* the
pages of the book began turning to liquid gold. This
was the first time I was completely speechless. Nana
said that the gold reflected onto my face and made me
look immaculate. I finished the word *room* and closed

my journal. I would write of my experiences in the throne room when we returned.

"Lynne, there are actually several ways we could get to the throne room. We could walk, ride the bus, ride on the train, fly in an airplane, or we could simply think it so and immediately our body and spirits would arrive there. What would you like to do?"

"I think it would be fun to take the bus. Remember the time you, Mom, Joe, Kevin, Grandma Alvina, and I took the bus to downtown Chicago? I remember we stayed the whole day. We had lunch in that fancy restaurant and went shopping and then rode the bus back home again."

"Yes, I remember that day, Lynne. It was wonderful. Let's make more memories and take another bus ride."

When the bus arrived, I began laughing. It was an odd looking bus. It was shaped like an egg and painted a vivid blue with big gold rings surrounding the letter E. Written across the front of this unusual vehicle, in bright yellow, was a sign that read, "Welcome to Eternity."

We stepped on the bus, and the driver greeted us with a big smile and said hello to Nana. He then looked at me and said, "Hello, Lynne, I'm so happy to see you. My name is Theophilus, but you can call me Theo."

"How do you know my name?" I asked. He winked at me as he answered.

"I know your name, and I knew you would be riding my bus today. I know everyone who rides my bus."

Nana told me this nice bus driver was a friend of the apostle Luke. Theo was a Roman citizen who became a friend of Luke's many, many years ago. I asked Theo if he would take me to see the apostle Luke sometime, and he answered, "I would be delighted to take you to Luke's house, and I'm sure Luke would be pleased to meet you as well."

There were men, women, and children of all ages on this interesting bus. Some had just arrived in this wonderful city, and others had been here a long time. We laughed and sang songs, and all too soon the bus stopped. Theo announced in a loud, happy voice, "All out for the throne room."

We had arrived in Zion, which sits at the top of a high hill in the largest section of heaven. As we stepped off the bus, I noticed Cara and Elnora were waiting for us. Elnora was Nana's guardian angel.

"I'm here to take you to the throne room," Cara said. "This is one of many places I will be staying with you. Elnora will be with Nana as well."

As we started toward the gathering place, I noticed the street was made of what looked like liquid gold, but it was not slippery. When I looked down at it, I could see what appeared as a shadow of my image. I knew this could not be because there was no darkness here, so how could there be a shadow?

I asked Cara, "How come I can see a shadow?"

"It is not a shadow, Lynne. What you saw was the Holy Spirit. If a person sees what they believe to be a shadow, it means they are paying attention. And that is a good thing because God wants us to always be aware of his Spirit covering us with his love."

Everywhere I turned, I could see thousands and thousands of angels and people. And I realized I knew everyone's name. I was able to feel the passion that filled heaven with a magnetic energy. The angels were like heavenly conductors transmitting peace and love to the citizens of heaven. Combined with the passion of God's people and the love and peace flowing from the angels, it was like a power carrying a current of togetherness that pulled us to an even greater intimacy with God.

Just outside the big temple was a wide stream of crystal clear water that came from a river that spilled out from the throne room. Twelve stately trees of life, each with an unusual fruit hanging from its branches, stood on the sides of the flowing stream. As we passed by one of these remarkable trees, Cara reached up and picked a piece of fruit that was red in color. She told me to eat it and told me this was the fruit of our eternal God. "When you eat it," Cara explained, "God's word is planted in you, just as a seed is planted in the ground. As you grow, God's love and understanding will grow in you."

It tasted like chocolate in my mouth, and the delicious taste stayed with me long after I was done eating.

The temple had the shape of a huge cross. The foundation was made of gopher wood that was painted gold and embellished with diamonds positioned between rubies and emeralds that were placed to spell out the twelve names of God. The names represented how God reveals himself to us.

Elohim, my Creator; Jehovah, my Lord; El Shaddai, my Supplier; Adonai, my Master; Jehovah Jireh, my Provider; Jehovah Rophe, my Healer; Jehovah Nissi, my Banner; Jehovah Mikkadesh, my Sanctifier; Jehovah Tsidkenu, my Righteousness; Jehovah Shalom, my Peace; Jehovah Rohi, my Shepherd; and Jehovah Shammah, my Abiding Presence.

The building faced to the east with the entrance on the north. Attached to the front of the temple was a porch with gigantic white marble columns laced with gold and silver twisted metal rings. Standing on both sides of the gold steps were white robed cherubim guarding the way.

When Cara and I reached the top step, I noticed three large bronze basins lined with mirrors. These basins contained white hyssop flowers floating in water. The smell reminded me of a bouquet of flowers mixed with mint. We stopped and washed our hands for the second time. The hyssops' white flower petals remained intact, no matter how many came for cleansing.

Upon entering the most holy place, I immediately became aware of another sweet smell. This time it reminded me of cedar trees. As we entered, the room became more of a covering than a dwelling. Solid gold walls surrounded see-through crystal curtains that sparkled with delicate stitches of colored thread. The threads came together to make pictures that looked like flowers, angels, and beautiful birds. Cherubim, iridescent cedar trees, and high columns lined the edge of the crystal clear gold floor. The room was bright with the light and glory of God the Father. Once again my nose became filled with a cloud of sweet smelling fragrance. My senses were bursting with delight, and my mouth was still fresh with the sweetness from the fruit I had eaten earlier.

Hundreds of angels flew around the room, singing, "Holy, holy, holy, worthy is the Lamb of God."

I felt God's unconditional love cover my body like a warm winter coat. If Cara had not been holding my hand, I would have fallen down from the beauty of worship and love.

On the south side of the room were seven large oil lamps of pure gold that represented the seven spirits of God. The number seven is the number of completeness. God is complete with the spirit of power, wisdom, understanding, counsel, might, knowledge, and fear.

The lamps burned continually on pure olive oil. Alongside the oil lamps rested several magnificent purple jars filled with spices and oils. A lamp stand called a menorah, was made of solid gold and shaped like a tree, had been placed toward the left side of the holy place. Six branches of the menorah were equally set, with three of the branches on each side arched upward, with one branch positioned in the middle. The tips of the branches held bowls shaped like almonds. On the north side of the room, a pure white table held two rows of twelve cakes of unleavened bread that had been made from pure fine flour. Next to the bread were three large clear pitchers of pure water.

Angels stood close by protecting golden bowls full of incense, which were the prayers of saints. Cherubim guarded several ruby-colored bottles filled with the tears of saints since the beginning of time. Two leather-bound books with raised gold letters had been placed on a white marble pedestal. The first was the book of prayers and good works of God's people, called the Book of Remembrance, which had been placed to the right of the second book, called the Book of Eternal Life. Every individual that resides in heaven had his or her name written in this book.

Looking toward the eastern end of the room, I could see a long tapestry made of white linen, with shades of silver reflecting the love of God. In front of the curtain, which separated the holy place from another area, was a square golden box with a solid gold crown resting on the top. Inside the box, incense mixed with salt burned continually.

Bordered by a flesh-colored silk curtain that had been torn from top to bottom and had been pulled back on both sides and tied with red and gold threads were three white marble steps leading up to the holy of holies. The hem of the curtain rested on the clear golden floor in the form of a brilliant precious stone.

Cara told me this was the only way to enter the holy of holies. As soon as we stepped into this celestial sphere, I noticed that on the sides of the tapestry stood four cherubim with wings so big they formed an archway surrounding the entire space. The cherubim honored the most holy piece of furniture in heaven, the ark of God. The ark was an oblong chest made of arcadia wood and overlaid with gold, both inside and out. It measured three and three quarter feet by two and one quarter feet by two and one quarter feet. On the top of the ark, two cherubim made of hammered gold sat on each end facing each other and looking toward the covering. With their wings arched gracefully up, the cherubim gently embraced this cherished ark of God.

Placed directly in front of the ark were two pieces of stone called the tables of testimony. Next to the inscribed stones sat a golden round pot filled with coriander seed, and positioned next to the pot was a solid brown stick that had blossoms of ripe almonds on it. This was the rod that belonged to a man named Aaron, and the filled vessel represented eternal life. The inscribed stones told us of the character of God. He is faithful and true, holy and righteous, jealous and compassionate. As we were taking in the splendor of this incredible room, I could hear the sound of angels' wings as they filled the room with heavenly music.

On the right side and in front of the ark, twenty-four men called elders were seated in a semi-circle. The armchairs were made of crystal and had topaz stones along the edges. The elders, dressed in garments of white with blue fringe on the corners of their sleeves and blue fringe at the edging of the hem, had on their heads gold crowns that were covered with rubies and emeralds.

Standing on royal pedestals, directly behind of the elders, stood twenty-four angels dressed in pure white robes. A luminous arc surrounded the entire area. In the center of the elders was the throne of his holiness. A thick red carpet led up to the throne that shone like an unbroken rainbow full of power and untold color.

Our Father's brilliance was almost blinding, and yet I could see his pure expression of love in all of his magnificence. His chair was made of intricately carved solid gold, with a quilted purple cloth that covered the high back and the triangular-shaped seat. Father was covered in a brilliant royal blue robe. A diadem resembling earth rested on the top of his head. On his broad shoulders, he had accepted all humanity since the beginning of time.

Sitting directly on the Father's right side was Jesus Christ, his Son. The Son's chair was made of solid silver, and the seat and back of his chair was draped in pure white linen with silver threads running through the spotless fabric. Jesus was wearing a flawless, pure white robe. Engraved on his forehead were the written words *Lord of lords*, and on his right thigh was a band of pure gold with the words *King of kings*. In his right hand, Jesus was holding a grand book shaped like a sword with seven bright stars extending into the space above.

The Holy Spirit circled over, covering the worshippers with truthfulness and power. This was truly hallowed ground. This was the throne of Almighty God.

Cara and I started up the red carpet. With our eyes filled with tears of happiness and our hearts expressing gratefulness, we fell to our knees with our heads lowered. Reverently, we worshiped the Father, Son, and Holy Spirit. The glory of the Lord filled the room with a powerful yet gentle wind. A reddish-orange smoke settled on us and filled us with understanding. The eternal beauty of the word of God is forever.

I do not remember removing my shoes, but it was then I noticed they had disappeared, and my white gown seemed to glow as if every fiber was in worship to God the Father, God the Son, and God the Holy Spirit. A holy silence overcame the room as I felt the nail-scarred hands of Jesus on my head. He spoke to me. His voice was like none other. Loud as thunder but soft as a whisper, "Lynne, I love you."

With every breath, I was taking in his love for me. I was filled with unspeakable joy. God is forever in absolute control of heaven and earth. It was then that one of God's angels came over to me and anointed me with the oil of gladness. From that instant, I have never had a moment of sadness.

The light and love that came from the throne was strong and powerful. The influence burned a tender passion into my soul. Full of compassion and love, God the Father smiled at me and said, "Lynne, I know your desire is to please me. Arise now and go about my kingdom. Take pleasure in every good thing I have given to you. I will join you here at my throne each new day at the worship hour."

I didn't want to move. For an unbroken time of worship, it seemed like only minutes before Cara touched my arm and spoke in a gentle tone. "Lynne, come now. We will come back tomorrow, and the next day, and every day after that. You will always be able to come to the throne room and worship. Do not forget that as we enjoy God's kingdom each new day we are also partaking in his love. Everything we say and everything we do is for his honor and for his glory."

I left my gift of thankfulness at the foot of the throne and said, "Thank you, Father, thank you, Jesus, and thank you, Holy Spirit, for loving me and allowing me to love you."

The Season of Gathering

To everything there is a season ...

Ecclesiastes 3:1 KJV

Cara and I were getting ready for the season of gathering festival. I was taking notes in my journal as she was telling me about all four seasons and festivals. This time the pages became a light green, similar to the happy color of eggs at Easter.

"We have four seasons, the season of gathering, the season of plenty, the season of purity, and the season of blessings. Remember the sound of trumpets blowing? They blow at the start of each new season."

"Yes, Cara, but it was a different sound I heard for the seventh hour."

"Yes, what you heard just before we went to the throne room was one long blast of a shofar. The shofar is different from the trumpets because it is made from the horn of a ram. The long blast reminds us that God is the one true God and he is the only One we are to worship."

"Where are the festivals held?"

"Remember the City of Zion? It is also called the city of festivals. For the first seven days of each season, the people of heaven assemble together for a time of jubilation. It is a moment in time when the citizens celebrate life with King Jesus."

Michael the Archangel presided over the season

of gathering festival. Families came dressed in special garments that represented their country. Musical instruments expressing love to our Lord were played as a parade of different cultures held flags high as they marched around the city. Costumes of every kind had multi-colored scarves and aprons with smocked shirts that were meticulously adorned. One gentleman from the land of the Incas was wearing a royal blue shawl over a red blouse with colorful braiding and gold fringe on the shawl and sleeves of his blouse. His jewelry was made from the bark of the kapok tree, and on his head he wore a Maskai Pache crown. It had four bands of braided gold rope with a large gold coin in the middle, with three long and one short blue and orange feather attached to the metal coin. In his right hand he held a staff of golden corn with gold tassels that represented his gift from God. The flag of his country had three wide vertical stripes. A white band in the middle represented peace, and one red stripe on either side indicated the shed blood of Jesus Christ. A coat of arms was sewn onto the center of the flag and displayed a shield bearing a llama, a cinchona tree, and a yellow cornucopia spilling out gold coins. The three icons were framed with a green wreath.

Long tables covered with pure white linens were decorated and set in place for the festivities. On each table, beside luscious grapes and pomegranates, large apricot apples sat in cobalt blue baskets with solid gold handles. The apples and grapes reminded the citizens of how sweet the love of our Father truly is. These sweet tasting apricot apples were grown along the sides of the grapevines in perfect rows at a gigantic orchard on the edge of the city. Several people would pick this delicious citrus after it was fully ripened and make an exquisite perfume from the pulp. The fragrance was mixed with pure water from the eternal springs, and petals from calendula were added and then poured into copper washtubs. This potpourri was used for cleansing.

Also placed on each table were white bowls filled with wheat and barley loaves. Large white pitchers overflowing with pure, sweet milk were placed on the left side of each basket of fruit, and amber-colored bottles filled with pure honey were placed next to the baked bread. Spices and different kernels and nuts from every country were put into giant alabaster jars.

Additional tables were set with a variety of cuisines that had been prepared for the family of God. Unique foods representing each culture had been prepared three days before the great feast. The tables were chock-full of wonderful dishes. The American Indians prepared delicious fish and corn served with warm butter and jellies. Spiced Creole dishes made by the French sat alongside hardy German and Scandinavian stews with fine gravies and sauces. The people of Zimbabwe made sadza. It was made of cornmeal and served with vegetables. They also made a delicious candy made from papaya that the children found to be irresistible. People of Mexico made delicious beans and salads with chili frijoles and peppers. Swedish families brought wonderful sweet breads garnished with raisins and cinnamon, and people from Asia brought special delicacies made with bean sprouts and rice. The Dutch folks brought potato dumplings and streusels, and the people of Italy contributed pastas made from special wheat topped with red sauce. The Polish people provided cheese-filled dumplings, and those from Israel brought bagels and honey cakes that had been decorated with almonds. Delicious salsa with onions and purple potatoes embellished with parsley made by the Peruvian population were very tasty. Candied yams, biscuits, and corn bread were a usual treat made by the folks from the deep south of the United States of America.

After the food was arranged on the tables, our Lord welcomed us into his abiding presence. With heartfelt tenderness he blessed the citizens and then spoke with each guest.

His time with the children was important to him, and Jesus enjoyed telling stories to the children. On an enormous round and well-worn red floor covering with wide braided gold fringe, the children eagerly waited for Jesus to begin another inspiring story. I sat down with the children and listened to His story. Jesus told it like this:

"Once there was a little boy who wandered from his home. He was not going any place particular; he wasn't even sure who or what he was looking for. He just kept wandering. He climbed over steep hills and hiked though valleys covered with thick bushes and thorns. As he came upon a wooded area, he realized he had gone very far from his home and family. He started talking to himself. 'I'm lost; why did I stray so far? My father must be so worried. How will I ever find my way?' Staring straight ahead, the boy could see a crossroad just before the forest. As he stood there alone with his watery eyes fixed on the crossroad, he knew he must make a decision. One road led into the woods, one way had a very sharp curve, one had a slight bend, and one road looked as if it were very narrow but straight.

"For a while, the boy just stood staring and thinking. After careful consideration, the boy decided he would take the straight and narrow road. At first, the road was smooth and wide enough to walk on. But as the boy walked farther, the path seemed to reduce to almost nothing, and soon he noticed the road had water approaching the edges. 'Where did this water come from? My feet are getting wet,' he said to himself.

"As salty tears began rolling down his cold cheeks, the boy knew he was in danger of never finding his way home. His tears were coming so fast he could hardly see. The light was fading from the sky, and the water on the road was turning to mud. A cold wind from the north sent chills throughout the boy's body. Soon the darkness covered the sky as he continued talking to himself. 'Where is the light that shines so brightly in the sky when I'm at home with my father?' The wind started howling so loud that it made the boy cry even more. Not knowing his father had been watching him and keeping close to his son, the boy cried out, 'Father, Father, I need your help.'

"Now the father, who had been standing directly behind his son, called to him, 'Son, I'm here.' But it was so dark and so windy and the boy was so full of fear that he never heard his father calling. It wasn't until the father reached out and embraced his son that the boy realized he was safe.

"'Father, you found me!' exclaimed the boy.

"'Son, I always knew where you were. It was you who thought you were lost,' answered the father. The father then picked his little boy up, gave him a big hug, and carried him all the way home.

"As the small boy lay safely in the father's arms, he looked up into his father's gentle eyes and whispered, 'Thank you, Father, for loving me. Forgive me for straying so far from home.'

"And his father replied immediately, 'Son, you are forgiven. Know that my love for you will never end.'"

When Jesus finished his story, children were hugging him and kissing his cheeks, and others were hanging on his robe. I asked him, "Jesus, just how much do you really love me?"

He stretched his arms out wide so I could see his nail-scarred hands. And with a love so powerful I could actually feel it from the top of my head to the tips of my toes, he smiled and said, "This much!"

After this time of fellowship, we were ready to enjoy a meal with our king. Cara and I thanked him for his love and goodness and delighted in him as we took pleasure in a galaxy of delicious foods.

Jesus Loves the Little Children

> ...Let the little children come to me, and do not
> hinder them, for the kingdom of heaven belongs to
> such as these.
>
> Matthew 19:14 NIV

"Lynne," Cara said, "I would like to show you a place filled with extraordinary rooms."

"What kind of place? Can I bring my journal?"

"Of course you may bring your journal. Put it in your purse and take my hand and close your eyes, and then imagine a beautiful red door."

The minute I opened my eyes I saw the most magnificent red door. The door was made from a solid red ruby that glistened with small, shiny diamonds, and the doorknob was actually a big, pure white rose.

"This is the special room where the angels keep watch over the souls of babies before they are conceived on earth."

When Cara opened the beautiful red door, I could see angels dressed in red and white gowns. They seemed to be suspended all around the room. They were holding small objects that had the form of small white doves.

"These doves represent the souls of the babies I told you about."

"Cara, was I ever one of those small doves?"

"Yes, every human soul began right here in this room."

"This is the most beautiful room I have ever seen!"

"Lynne, see the angel nearest the blue window. She is holding your baby brother. Jesus told me your baby brother would be departing to earth for a short stay. Soon you will be going with Jesus to bring your mother a message. Now, Lynne, I will show you another room. Turn around and tell me what you see now."

"I see a crystal clear door. I'm not sure if that's pink or yellow."

"That because it's made of topaz. The door was originally yellow, but because of its warmth, it changes its color to appear pink."

As Cara pushed open the door, she began explaining, "The inside of the room has a different meaning to every person who enters. Immediately after a child is conceived on earth, God instructs the earth parents to love and care for his little one until the time comes when he sends his angels to bring his chosen one home. Sometimes it is for a very short time."

"Just like me?"

"Yes, Lynne, just like you."

"Can we go inside now?"

As the door opened, I immediately recognized this special room. It was the same room where I first met Adele and Bella.

"Will my brother be coming to this room too?"

"Yes, but not right now. When it is his time to come to this room, John Michael will have his own guardian angel, and he will meet with you after he arrives here. Lynne, I will show you one more door, but you must enter this door alone. Close your eyes and think of something that makes you happy."

"That will be easy, Cara."

I shut my eyes and was surprised when I opened them. This door didn't look like any door I had ever seen. It reminded me of the sky in Michigan, and white wavy lines seemed to be coming out and through the inside of it. As I walked slowly closer to this unusual door, I began to hear the sound of seagulls, and the scent of water filled my nose. And then I realized that the door was actually a passageway.

"Lynne," Cara called out, "when you step through the door, you will see Jesus."

As soon as I entered the passageway, I could feel his presence.

Immediately, Jesus spoke to me. "Lynne, we will bring your mother a message from our Father, and the spirit of your brother, John Michael, will also go with us. It will be during the season of blessings. We will leave at 3:00 a.m. earth time. Our journey will be incredible. I will place John Michael in your arms, and I will carry you both. The three of us will float down a path of puffy clouds linked together like a string of big white pearls. We will arrive at the bedroom of your parents at exactly 3:12 a.m. that morning."

"Your mama will wake the instant we enter her room. We will enter with a light shining so brightly even you will be surprised. The light will not wake your dad. This will be a special time just for your mama. Our Father will be showing his love for her, and you will tell her that sometimes in life things happen that people do not understand. But she must learn to love and trust God through it all. Your mama will not know she is six weeks pregnant.

"John Michael will be wrapped in a small, blue blanket, and he will feel light in your arms. I will tell you to put your baby brother down gently at my feet.

The three of us will wait until your mama adjusts her eyes and ears so she will know this is not a dream. I will then tell you to speak to your mother. You will tell her very soon your baby brother will be born on earth, and soon after he will return to live in the kingdom of God. You will tell her this was planned from the beginning of time. Before we leave her, you will tell her that you love her and you're happy because one day we will all live together in eternity.

"Then the room will become dark. Your mama will have tears, and she will keep looking to the corner of the room long after we're gone. But I promise you, Lynne, she will feel better, and you will see her again.

"Your brother, John Michael, will be born on earth July 22, 1974. He will come to live with us in my kingdom on November 15, 1975."

As I walked back through the door, I could hear beautiful words coming from above.

Jesus loves me, this I know, for the Bible tells me so.

Little ones to him belong, they are weak, but he is strong.

Jesus loves me, he who died,

Heaven's gates to open wide; he will wash away my sin,

Let his little child come in.

Jesus loves me, loves me still. Though I'm very weak and ill.

From his shinning throne on high,

Comes to watch me where I lie.

Jesus loves me; he will stay

Close beside me all the way.

Then his little child will take,

Up to heaven for his dear sake.

"Cara, what are those beautiful words I heard as I left the room?"

"They are the words of a poem that was written by a lady named Anna Warner. And a man called William Bradbury set the lovely words to music. Those words bring great comfort to your mother and family, and it is also a favorite at The Concert of the Angels."

Cara and I walked away singing, "Jesus loves me, this I know…"

As we were singing, I knew I would soon write of this incredible experience on royal blue pages.

Season of Blessings

… Blessed are those you choose and bring near to live in your courts.

Psalm 65:4 NIV

It was the first time I had experienced the season of blessings, and the air was full with the anticipation of the great feast. Nana told me that I could help her bake small cakes made with figs and almonds. She said we would be using her favorite recipe.

"Lynne, did you know the fig was the first fruit of this season?"

"No, I didn't. The only thing I know about figs is Grandpa ate little square cookies called Fig Newtons."

"Yes, he did, and he certainly did enjoy them. Figs grow on tall trees that spread out over fifty feet in diameter. The leaves of the fig trees are so large and strong they are used to make clothing."

"They must be really big leaves."

"Unlike other fruit, the figs are picked gradually because they do not ripen all at the same time. They were never-ending and their tiny colorful flowers form large clusters on giant branches before the figs start to grow. Once the figs develop and ripen, they are delicious."

"Can they be eaten as soon as we pick them?"

"Yes, and sometimes I dry them and press them

into cakes that taste like Fig Newtons! The flesh of the fig is sweet, and the sap of the tree smells like fresh milk and could also be used in baking. If you are ready to help me bake the cakes, you better get your journal. You can write down the recipe."

I took down Nana's favorite recipe, and now the page was the color of figs.

2 1/2 cups flour

1/2 cup ground almonds

1/2 teaspoon baking powder and ground cinnamon

1/4 teaspoon ground allspice and salt

1 1/4 cups sugar

1/2 cup oil

2 eggs

1/2 cup orange juice

1 cup finely chopped figs

Mix together flour, ground almonds, baking powder, cinnamon, allspice, and salt. Beat together sugar and oil until light and fluffy. Add eggs and beat. Mix and add orange juice and bake for 35 minutes in a 350° oven.

When the cakes were done, we cooked a special cream made from sweet flowers and whipped it together with the juice from pomegranates to make an unusual frosting. We decorated the cakes with delicate pastel-colored flower petals.

I had just finished putting the last of the colored petals on one of the cakes when Nana said, "Lynne, I think that is Elizabeth at the window."

Elizabeth always has something very important to report. She always gives news about those who are coming to live in the kingdom.

"Hello, Elizabeth, come in and see what Lynne and I are making for the banquet."

The first thing I became aware of as Elizabeth stepped into the kitchen was her long white robe. It was made of pure silk with hundreds of small diamonds shining brilliantly within the threads. Her hair was the color of the wheat that glistens in the field, and her slender figure reminded me of the hourglass that sat on Nana's shelf. She smiled at me, and her eyes were full of delight as she spoke. "Lynne, you, Nana, and Cara should go to the entrance gate this morning and keep watch. Someone very close to you will be arriving soon."

We arrived at the gate, and I could see Jesus standing just the other side of the threshold. Next to him was a tall angel with long arms and the hands of a giant. This strange-looking angel was hovering directly over my brother, John Michael. He was holding a twisted and distorted entity. As I stared with amazement, Cara explained what was actually taking place. "Because nothing that is unpleasant or harmful may enter into heaven, this angel, who is called Gevariah, has purged all of the sickness that was inside your brother's small body. After John Michael's body is free from all disease, Jesus will carry your brother over the threshold."

"Cara, where is Gevariah taking that thing?"

"There is an enclosed space called Netherworld, where all harmful matter and evil spirits must be taken. Everything in Netherworld is burned to an intense heat and remains there for eternity."

The three of us watched as Jesus' loving arms picked up my brother and carried him into heaven. Thoughts of that October day when I walked through those massive gates and Jesus carried me across that same threshold filled my soul. Now, my little brother, John Michael, a child of only sixteen months in earth years, was accepting that same joy. I couldn't wait until I could show my brother our house and all of our animals and the wonderful garden we shared with our cousin. We would have so much fun together.

"Cara, will John Michael be joining us now?"

"Not now, Lynne. John Michael will first meet his guardian angel, and his angel will bring him to meet us soon. It won't be very long."

School of the Holy Trinity

No longer will a man teach his neighbor or a man his brother saying know the Lord; because they will all know me ...

Jeremiah 31:34 NIV

I asked Cara to take me to the Way of Truth Center located on Main Street. Cherubim watched over and cared for the center that was shaped like a tall evergreen tree. Made of solid green marble, the sides connected with solid gold chains that formed the shape of the emerald triangle. The building was constructed on a square foundation made of twelve layers of ebony and limestone. The names of the twelve tribes of Israel had been engraved into the layers with metallic blue copper. The bottom layer was engraved with the name of Benjamin and continued on up with Manasseh engraved at the next to bottom layer, then Ephraim, Judah, Issachar, Zebulun, Ruben, Simeon, Gad and Naphatali, Asher, and the name of Dan on the top layer.

Because I had left earth at an early age, there was plenty I had not yet learned. I always liked books, and there were oodles of books I was looking forward to reading. I wanted to know of the life of Jesus as a child. My Sunday school teacher, Miss Goldie, told me Jesus loved me so much that he gave his life for me. But now I wanted to know more. What did Jesus do as a young boy? What color was his favorite? And what games did he play when he was young? Did he have brothers and sisters, and what were their names? What was the name of the school he attended, and who was his best friend when he was in the third grade? What stories did his mom read to him, and which story did he like the best?

Inside this huge library of books were twelve floors of discovery, separated by areas of sitting rooms that spread outward like branches of a tree. A large glass elevator allowed visitors to observe different seating areas. Each one unlike the other in color and arrangement, the areas had been designed with a theme from the word of God.

"Cara, let's go to one of the sitting rooms. It seems like a good place for me to write in my journal."

"Sure, Lynne, I like the blue room with the big easy chairs where I can put my feet up. I think I will read my new book while you're writing."

"Look, Cara, my pages are turning the color of peaches. I'm so amazed every time I begin writing."

"Lynne, even though this is the blue room, your pages turned to a soft orange color because it is so peaceful here."

The first floor of the learning center was most significant. The walls were covered with colorful mosaic tiles and engraved in Aramaic script. Books of great importance lined shelves of solid gold. Cara told me the books had been skillfully labeled and numbered and then listed in alphabetical sequence.

Inside a very unique room, called the Missed Blessings Room, were hundreds of polished metal boxes of different sizes and shapes. Stored in rows, in alphabetical sequence according to first names, the labeled boxes contained paper similar to sheepskins. On each paper was written a blessing that God wished to give to his people while they were still living on earth. Because of their lack of faith, people just never asked God to bless them. So, here sat countless boxes of blessings, unclaimed.

On the east end of the top floor was a great room. Written on the entrance door to this room were purple and gold letters that spelled out The Restful Room. Windows reaching from the floor to the ceiling were made of diamond blue glass. Pure white flowers covered light purple walls. All around the room were angels dressed in white and purple robes that continually sang soft sounds of comfort. Comfortable easy chairs with lavender-filled cushions bordered this peaceful rest area, and a thoughtful stillness overcame the entire room.

Chairs were placed so that no matter which one you chose you would be able see your special view from the window. Once you were seated in the chair of your choice, the beautiful window in front of you would open up, and the view would be anything you could imagine it to be. The first time I sat in one of these special chairs, I watched angels floating in an aqua colored sky. Among the angels were pictures of my family. Connected to each portrait was a tiny book with dates engraved in gold. These dates indicated their day of birth on earth and the date each one would enter heaven.

As I sat thanking God for this beautiful vision and wondering when I would be able to peek down and see them, I heard Bella say, "Lynne, now that you have seen the pictures of your family, would you like

Adele and I to show you how you can see what they are doing at this very minute?"

"Bella, Adele, when did you get here?"

"Oh, we have been watching you enjoy your family and thought this would be the perfect time for you to learn how to play 'peek-a-boo'!"

"Adele, it's not peek-a-boo! It is actually a method by which the people of heaven can see those they love who are not living here."

"Well, I like to call it peek-a-boo. What do you think, Lynne?"

"I agree with you Adele; peek-a-boo sounds curious and fun!"

Bella was smiling as she said, "Okay, we'll call it peek-a-boo if that makes you both happy. Now let me explain to Lynne how it is done. Lynne, you must indicate the person or persons you would like to see by touching their picture. When your hand comes in contact with the picture, you are expressing your desire to see that person. You will be able to see them by an invisible energy. It's like watching a movie. You can see and hear the people in the film, but they cannot see or hear you. However, they will be aware of your presence."

As she walked to the open window, Bella reached out to touch the pictures and asked me, "Who is it that you would like to see first?"

It only took me a second to answer. "My brothers and sisters. Yes, I would love to see what they are doing."

At the same moment Bella laid her hand on the pictures, the pictures lit up and began swirling into one another. I could see Joe's picture, and then Kevin's and then Carol Ann's and Jeanne's. They went around and around until all I could see was a whirlpool of colors. It looked like a giant lollipop in the middle of a lightning storm.

"Lynne, concentrate on what you want to see as you're watching the circle of colors," said Bella.

"It's going so fast, Bella. The pictures are disappearing."

Adele was so excited she yelled, "Watch closely, Lynne!"

And then before I could say another word, I saw planets and stars and clouds flying by. Then a brilliant beam of light flashed before me, and I could see five people in the yard of a home I didn't recognize. They were laughing and running, and it seemed there was water everywhere. As they ran I could see Joe with a blue water balloon. He was about to throw it at Jeanne when it burst. What he didn't know was Jeanne was laughing, not because his balloon burst but because she had a big red balloon and was getting ready to throw it at him!

I spotted Carol Ann. She had a great big water gun and was pumping it up, getting ready to squirt Kevin, but she was too late. His water gun was bigger and he was faster as he doused her, and they both laughed hysterically as she yelled, "I'll get you back!"

Then I saw a girl with long yellow hair. She was sitting in a lawn chair laughing as she watched my brothers and sisters. I wondered why she wasn't throwing balloons or squirting water. Then I saw her head tilt upward toward the heavens. She was smiling, and I knew she could feel my happiness.

"Bella, who is the pretty girl with the long yellow hair, and why isn't she running and playing?"

"Lynne, that lovely girl is a special friend of your

brothers and sisters. She has been sick for a long time and is not able to run or play. Your brothers and sisters go to her house every day because they know it makes her happy. Soon she will be your new friend, Lynne, and when she is here with us, she will be able to run and play, and her legs will be as good as new."

"I'm sure I will like my new friend when she arrives. I'm so glad my sisters and brothers make her happy. I think I have the best brothers and sisters ever! And someday my family will be here with me to share the love of our holy God, and I can't wait!"

Although there was a wealth of information at the learning center, Cara suggested I also attend a class at school.

I signed up for Knowing Him 101 at Holy Trinity School. It was on this first day of school that I met another one of my beautiful cousins.

Cara and I had started along the pathway that led to the school grounds when we noticed Jesus coming toward us. Immediately he began speaking. I felt surrounded in his love as I listened to his words. "I am happy you are looking forward to school, Lynne. Listen carefully to the instructor and be sure to have fun as you learn."

Then he took my hand and placed it in his hand as he continued speaking. "Now, there is something I want you to do for me. I want you to take the path to the next crossroad. At the end of the road is a posted signboard. Follow the arrow pointing to the south. At the end of the road will be someone awaiting your arrival."

I felt his hand gently disappear from mine, and just like that he was gone. I was filled with excitement. I knew I had just been blessed. When Jesus asks us to do something for him, it is always because he takes such pleasure in seeing his children happy.

I was almost running, and Cara was laughing as she said, "Lynne, slow down. God's promise will be waiting exactly where he said it would be." We came to the end of the road, and there was the signpost. An arrow pointing to the south, just like he said. Turning south, we continued on. It wasn't long before I could see an unfamiliar vista of different colors gleaming in the distance. A mountain appeared to be wearing a perfectly white, oval-shaped hat that had a pink glow about it. At the foot of the mountain was what seemed to be an ice pond. Hundreds of honey-colored trees with their branches directed upward like loving arms gave praise to our Father. Blue and yellow flowers surrounded the entire area. As we continued onward, we could see the pond was actually made of pure diamonds reflecting the mountain above and everything below. Along the edge of this diamond pond were beveled ridges that formed a crest around a strand of large white flowers with waxy green leaves tumbling down on a gold vine. Beneath the vine were small purple herbs. The aroma of lavender mixed with the scent from the white gardenias filled the area with sweetness. Set against the warm, bright blue sky, it was an enchanting view.

Dancing in the center of this majestic scene was a most extraordinary girl. A white chiffon gown reached just below her knees, and pink ribbons wrapped around her delicate ankles held beautiful silk slippers on her feet. Her long, soft brown hair hung gracefully beneath a wreath of laurel that matched the softness of her green eyes. A smile on her sweet face expressed the joy within her. With her elbows rounded softly upward and her hands elegantly relaxed, she seemed to be an exquisite painting that had come to life. She looked as though she was suspended from an invisible wire as she waltzed across the sparkling pond.

Cara and I stood in awe of her as she gracefully twirled around and around. The mountains and trees responded in song as they joined her with a melody of love. Appealing to our emotions as well as our eyes, without words, the girl was communicating the passion of Christ. She was telling of the everlasting love of our Lord and Savior. It was the most beautiful ballet ever.

Near the closing of the dance, the girl became aware of Cara and me. She smiled, and we could see the glory of God shining within her. Now I understood. This extraordinary girl was God's promise. This was the beginning of our relationship, and throughout eternity, Misty and I would remain two special friends who were introduced exclusively by God.

It wasn't by chance that Misty had also signed up for Knowing Him 101. Misty's special angel, Flora, reminded me a little of Adele. She was always laughing. The four of us began to sing and dance, and before long, Flora and Cara began chatting because Misty and I kept changing the words to the song. "Misty, I'm so glad we're friends and will be going to school together."

"I'm happy that God introduced us, and I think Flora and Cara are quite pleased too!"

When we arrived for class, I was surprised to see so many people at the school. There had to be at least three thousand people. Classes were held outside in a beautiful meadow. Grown-ups as well as little people gathered around as we waited for our instructor. The ground was soft like a pillow made of green, goose down feathers. Energetic birds and brightly colored flowers flew like little kites all around us as soft music echoed in our ears.

Our instructor appeared, and we all bowed to praise him. The teacher for this group of students was Jesus!

Jesus began by telling us how happy he was we were here to learn more about him. Our ears were tuned to the sound of his voice. When he spoke, we listened carefully. His authoritative yet gentle voice gave peace and understanding to all. I could see and feel the gentleness and compassion in him. His eyes were full of love. It was as if he was looking at each one of us separately.

He made me feel as if I was the only one there with him. All of the students honored him with a prayer of thanks, and together we sang, "Thank you, Lord," in perfect harmony. Our wonderful Savior then began to tell us of his life.

At the same moment Jesus began talking, Cara whispered "Lynne, your journal." And immediately I reached in my purse. As soon as I put the pencil to the cloth, it turned the loveliest shade of red.

"I am my father's son. I am the second person of the Trinity. My father's word became flesh when I was born on earth in a small city located about six miles south of Jerusalem."

He told us his mother's name was Mary, and one day, as Mary was resting from her everyday chores, the angel Gabriel appeared and spoke to her.

"Greetings, Mary. Do not be afraid. My name is Gabriel, and I bring good news. God wants to bless you. Tonight, while you are sleeping, the Holy Ghost will visit you, and you will conceive a son. His name shall be called Jesus, and he will be a Savior to his people."

Jesus continued, "My mother loved God, but she wondered why she had been chosen for such a big responsibility. Why had God chosen an ordinary girl like her to carry out his plan for the salvation of his people? She questioned if her mother and father would believe what had happened to her. She had just become engaged to marry Joseph, and now she was unsure if he too would understand. For several days, my mother could think of nothing else. As she went about her daily chores, she prayed. She prayed in the morning, she prayed at the noon hour, and she prayed in the evening. And then one evening, as she was praying, the thought came to her that she should visit her cousin. Mary knew Elizabeth would be happy to see her, and my mother knew Elizabeth's understanding of the Scriptures would bring comfort to her. My grandparents gave their permission, and soon Mother set out on a journey to the hills surrounding Jerusalem. Elizabeth and her husband lived about a five-day walk from the town of Nazareth, where my mother lived. As Mother approached their home, she heard Elizabeth cry out, 'Mary, welcome! I'm so pleased to see you.'

"Elizabeth was also going to have her own child soon, and she was thankful Mother would be with her. Together, my mother and Elizabeth called upon God the Father, and they prayed and fasted for three days. At the end of the third day, my Heavenly Father gave them both peace and understanding. They knew our Father had a special plan for their lives. Father God told Elizabeth she was about to be the mother of a baby boy, and she would name him John. My mother would also give birth to a boy child, and this child would be the Christ. My earthly father, Joseph, and my mother soon married. As her time to give birth drew closer, my mother remembered the scriptures her parents had read to her as a child. The book of Isaiah told of the birth of Christ and his kingdom."

Jesus continued, "My mother and father were Israelites who descended from King David. Near the time my mother was to give birth, my parents had to travel from their hometown of Nazareth to the small town Bethlehem. This was because the Roman Empire decided all Israelites had to report to Bethlehem to be counted. The town was so small, and crowds of people could be found on the streets searching for rooms to stay the night. When my parents entered Bethlehem, they could not find a place to stay. One innkeeper was kind enough to tell them there was a place near the shepherd's field. It would at least give them shelter for the night. He told them animals were in the shelter, but he believed they would be safe. Joseph was thankful he had a place for Mary to rest. As they entered the small, wooded shelter Joseph noticed some hay piled in a corner. He took a bundle of the sweet smelling hay and with the blanket that lay on his donkey made a bed for my mother. Then he took a horse trough and filled it with hay to make a crib for the baby.

"That same night, under the light of a star that shone brightly in the eastern sky, my mother gave birth to her firstborn son and laid me in the crib. In this small sanctuary, my parents thanked God and christened me Jesus as wooly sheep, wide-eyed cows, a camel, and my father's donkey stood watch. Before long, shepherds came from the fields, and wise men came from far away. Everyone brought gifts and worshipped the Christ child, the son of Joseph and Mary."

Jesus told the class of his mother's emotions. How much she loved her baby. She knew this sweet baby she carried in her womb and now cuddled in her arms would one day be her Savior. He said it was too much for her to comprehend. She wondered how she would be able to tell her child he was the one who formed the earth. He was the one who placed the stars in the heavens and filled the seas with fish. What words should she use to tell him he was the only begotten son of the one true God? That he is one with the Father and the Holy Spirit.

God entrusted her to teach his Son about the everyday responsibilities and pleasures of life and she knew it would not be long before her son would be taken from her. She would have to believe in God to give her the strength and courage to face each day. She would have to accept the truth of God's word and live each day with a positive attitude.

Jesus told us, "As the years passed and I grew, my mother taught me how to walk and speak respectfully, and of course to have fun. She fed me fruits and vegetables to help my body grow strong, and she taught me to play the harp. We sang and laughed and read scriptures and prayed to our Heavenly Father."

He told us Mary made sure she gave him a big hug and told him how much she loved him every day. He said both Joseph and Mary practiced truthfulness, compassion, and unconditional love simply living each day by the word of God.

He also told us in the first month of every year the Feast of Passover was held in the town of Jerusalem. Although it was a two-day journey from his home in Nazareth, his earthly father, Joseph, and his family gladly attended this joyous feast every year.

The festival lasted for seven days, and on the sixth day each family would choose an unblemished lamb for their meal. They would then prepare for the meal by killing the lamb and roasting it over a pit of coals. Just before sunset on the seventh day, all of the people would come together for the meal and give thanks to God for the deliverance of Israel from slavery in Egypt.

The meal was called Seder, which means Order of the Service, and it began with everyone seated at a beautifully set table. The dishes and pans used for serving at this exclusive occasion would be used exclusively for the Seder meal. A set of gold candlesticks held seven candles, and a golden goblet filled with the finest wine was placed on each table. In the center of every table was a large white bowl filled with salt water symbolizing the tears of the Hebrew people. White linen napkins held unleavened bread and were set at each individual place setting along with a small blue bowl, a pitcher of water, and a hand towel. Before the meal, the candles would be lit, and the priest would tell the biblical story of the exodus of God's people.

The congregation would then wash their hands, and all would join in for the blessing over the food. The lamb, which had been roasted earlier, was served with bitter herbs. Eggs that had been boiled and roasted were also served, and a sweet mixture of apples and figs completed the meal.

The year he turned twelve, his family had attended the feast as usual. Soon after the meal, they were headed back to Nazareth with some neighbors. After a few hours of walking, Joseph decided his family needed a short rest. They were gathered together for a drink of water when Mary realized Jesus was not with the family. His brothers and sisters called out his name, and Joseph asked the neighbors if anyone had seen him. It became clear to Mary that Jesus was nowhere in their group. As they started back to Jerusalem in search for Jesus, Joseph held his wife close and told her not to be troubled, to remember God is always in control.

After three days, Mary and Joseph found Jesus in the temple courtyard outside the House of the Book. Surrounded by his teachers, Jesus was listening to every word as they spoke. He would ask questions of them, and they were all astonished by his wisdom. He always answered the questions asked of him with a scripture. The spiritual leaders were surprised this twelve-year-old boy could discern and understand their traditions.

His parents were not so impressed. They were upset and hurt that he had been away for so long. Mary approached him first. "Son, where have you been all of this time? Your father and I have been searching and searching. Why did you not tell us you wanted to stay behind and talk with the temple teachers?"

As Joseph came close, Jesus could see his earthly

father was happy to see he was safe. Jesus spoke kindly as he said, "Mother and Father, why have you put yourselves to this trouble? Do you not know that I must be in my Heavenly Father's house? I must do the work of my Father."

With a smile on her face, his mother embraced him and with a hug answered, "Yes, now let's go home. Your brothers and sisters will be happy to see you."

Jesus obeyed and went back to Nazareth with them. But after this he became much wiser and stronger as he grew more pleasing to his Heavenly Father.

Mary knew Jesus must do the will of his Father. She thought to herself, *He will always be my child, but most importantly, Jesus is his Heavenly Father's son.* This ended my first day at school. Jesus closed the learning session with his face full of joy as he blessed us all and said, "Grow in love and know that my love passes all knowledge."

The Welcome Party

Misty and I took a walk and stopped for a while in a meadow flooded with beautiful pink and white roses alongside tiny blue flowers. In front of colored trees stood the largest oak tree I had ever seen. I took my journal from my purse when Misty asked, "Lynne, how come you are always writing in that beautiful book?"

"It's my assignment book. I must record all that I see and experience."

As I began to write about the beautiful field of flowers, the pages began to turn pink, and Misty asked, "Have you written anything about me?"

"Yes, Misty, remember when we first met and you were dancing on that diamond pond? I wrote how beautiful you looked and how God introduced us. And how we would be friends forever."

"That's so nice of you, Lynne. I'm going to write something about you in my diary."

"What's your assignment for this season?"

"Eldon gave me some special paints and told me I should make a painting for the next season of purity festival. I'm doing a drawing first, and then I will fill it in with the paints."

"What is it a picture of?"

"I cannot tell. It's going to be a surprise, but I can tell you that I know you will like it. When I brush the paint on the canvas, the paint color comes alive and the picture becomes animated."

"Wow, I can't wait until you're done. I think everything here is like magic was on earth. When I write in my journal, the pages turn different colors."

As Misty and I were talking, we noticed a man beneath the large oak tree. He seemed quite busy. Placed on the ground near the area he was working laid two piles of wood. One stack of wood was white, and the other was the color of cedar. Next to the wood was a coil of rope that at first glance looked like a large brown snake. We could hear the man as he whistled a melody that filled the air with cheerfulness. He was bent over a long section of wood and had a hammer in his left hand and two large nails resting on the edge of his lip.

Misty's green eyes sparkled as she remarked to me how much the man reminded her of her earthly father. "My dad liked to work with wood," she whispered. "I remember his favorite hammer. It had a red ring painted on the handle, and at the end of the handle was a piece of silver iron. The smooth side was used for striking nails into the wood, and the other side was a claw. The claw was used to pull out the nails that didn't go into the wood straight away."

He didn't hear us until we were standing directly behind him. "Excuse us, sir, can we be of some help?"

Without interrupting his work, he turned around and smiled. "Hello, girls. My name is Robert. Yes, I could use some assistance. I'm making a swing for my granddaughter. When we lived on earth, I made one for her in a field behind our house. She was so fond of it I decided to make another in this field. Her name is Patti, and she will be joining us today. If you girls would like to pick some pink roses and weave them into this hemp, I could use it for a cord to hang the swing from a large limb on this tree."

After we had gathered a basketful of pink roses, this kind man, Robert, showed us how to join them. We made a long chain of the roses, and Misty held one end of each length with the rose chain in the middle of the two ropes. As she held on to the three pieces, I began putting one strand over the other until the entire length was woven into a braid. Robert told us it was the most beautiful swing cord ever made. He was almost done making the swing when he began expressing his thoughts about Patti. We could feel his passion and excitement as he spoke of his special granddaughter.

"Before Patti became sick her long hair was the color of yellow taffy and her beautiful hazel eyes reflected the happiness within her. She was always singing and laughing and playing with her dogs. She loved all animals, but her dogs were her favorite. And then, one day, everything changed for Patti. Her strong body became frail. Her legs grew tired, and she could no longer walk and play with her beloved dogs. She became thin because she could not keep the food she ate in her stomach. Her yellow hair fell out because of the medicine she was given. Day after day, Patti became weaker and weaker because of a disease called cancer. Her cheerful smile began to vanish from her lovely face. She was so very tired of this disease. Early one morning, while she was talking with Jesus, Patti asked Jesus if he would send his angels for her. She knew it was time for her to go to her eternal home in heaven. Jesus answered Patti immediately and sent his angels for her."

It was then that Misty and I looked at one another and knew we both had the same idea. "Robert, Misty and I have an idea. We would like to give a welcome party for Patti."

With much enthusiasm, Robert said, "What an excellent idea!"

"This is just the place for a welcome party," I told Misty. "The rainbow-colored trees look so beautiful around Patti's swing."

"I know," said Misty. "She will also enjoy the blue and white birds that gather here. We can set up tables and chairs and cover them with fine lace and hang chains of white roses from each table and chair."

"Yes, this is just the right place. We will invite all of our friends. We can each bring a precious stone of our own and present them to her as a welcome home gift. We could set all of the jewels into a crown, and she could wear it on her head like a queen."

"Yes, and we will wrap the crown in a beautiful package," Misty said with a smile.

When Robert arrived with Patti and her guardian angel to the welcome party, I was so excited. "Misty, Patti is the girl I saw with my sisters and brothers when I peeked down at earth!"

"Isn't God good, Lynne? I wish your brothers and sisters could see her now. She is more lovely than Robert described. Her golden hair surrounds her sweet face and flows all the way down her backside. Her strong legs and body are now perfect in form, and Patti's lovable face mirrors the joy within her soul."

The angels came with their horns, flutes, and violins and played joyful music as we joined them in song and danced around the big oak tree.

Everyone joined in a game of croquet. Each player chose a woodwind instrument. The first player started by hitting a flower-covered round bubble though a series of shiny silver hoops. The player who hit the flower-ball through all of the hoops without bursting their bubble was the winner! The winner then had to play a silly tune by blowing air into or against the edge of the instrument, and the guests would try to name the tune. It was a game of cheering others on with lots of laughing.

Colorful birds flew all around us as we took turns on the lovely swing. We drank oodles of giggle tea served in big blue china cups and giggled until we were silly. Betty Jean served big slices of googleberry pie on golden plates. And a girl by the name of Alice, who wore shiny black shoes and a white apron over a blue dress, dished out pink bubblegum cake and gobs of chocolate ice cream in big strawberry cones. The cones were covered with rainbow sprinkles that tasted like every color imaginable.

It was time to present our special gift to Patti. Everyone gathered around as Patti carefully untied the candy ribbons and unraveled the gold fabric from which the gift was wrapped. Inside the beautiful wrapping was a clear glass box. Inside the box laid several precious jewels. There were diamonds, rubies, emeralds, and sapphires. They were all set perfectly onto a beautiful golden crown. Patti was beaming with joy as Misty placed the crown on Patti's head.

When the party came to a close, my friends and I were all happy we had given of our time and talents to a very special girl. Patti thanked us all and told us she especially liked the giggle tea. She hoped we could give her the recipe. We could see the joy in Patti's lovely face as she spoke. "Tomorrow I shall lay my crown of jewels at the feet of Jesus in the throne room." This made everyone so happy. We all sang praises to Jesus, our king.

After the party, Robert and Patti invited me to visit Patti's new residence. Patti and her grandfather lived on Malachi Road in the town of Gloryville. Patti's house was the color of a soft pink carnation with white gingerbread trim and a large pale yellow porch that wrapped around the entire place. It radiated an inviting aura. Rocking chairs made from white wicker with soft cherry cushions sat on the porch to welcome her family and friends.

When Patti first stepped through the door of her new home, she let out a shriek of delight. Her big eyes spotted three Irish wolfhound puppies waiting for her in the cozy, pastel living room. As the three dogs ran to meet her, she held her arms out wide to catch each one of them and then scooped them all up and cuddled them tight as she called them by name. "Easy, Caleb, Sammy, it's so good to see you." Patti and her dogs had an exceptional relationship. They did more than just play; they spoke to one another in a special language. Every word spoken is understood. They learn from one another, and she reads animal stories to them. Now she can play and talk with them for as long as she wishes. When I looked over at Robert, I could see and feel his gladness.

A New Beginning

...And I shall dwell in the house of the Lord
forever.

Psalm 23:6 KJV

Noble and I had been riding all morning when we
came to an open river valley. Between the two sides of
the narrow valley flowed water as blue as the sapphire
gems that embraced the foundation of heaven. The
water had a character of its own as it moved quietly
from south to north, as if it were resting from a long
journey. I could see several formations of rocks within
and out of the water. The outer perimeter of each large
stone was almost round in shape. But each had a different pattern, with layers of soil, rock, and colors
within their own circle. The creations that rested in
the water looked like animals that had been formed
and frozen in time.

Stones along the edge of the water had formed a
natural boundary. Tall, thick trees with low branches
brushed the gentle wind with their light and elegant
leaves.

I knew I was about to experience something very
important when Noble lowered himself so I would
dismount. We were both feeling the beauty of our
surroundings when I decided to take my journal from
Noble's saddlebag. Sitting on the cool grass near the
water's edge, I took my silver pencil and began to

write on the silver cloth of my journal. I was amazed when I wrote each word, because not only did the page not turn to another color, but the words themselves became a dazzling silver as well.

I heard the voice of a woman. I looked up to see a beautiful lady carrying a large white water jug. She strolled along the water's edge with the elegance of a queen. I noticed her long wavy hair was fastened with a jeweled clasp.

I waved my hand as to say hello to this charming woman and called out to her, "Hello, that pitcher must be very heavy."

"Oh, not at all," she said as she started toward us. "It is so nice to meet you. My name is Eve. I have a place just a short walk past the hill to the east. Why is it I have never seen you here before?"

"This is our first visit to this section of the kingdom. My name is Lynne, and this is Noble."

From the moment we started talking, I felt like I had known her forever. She seemed so motherly. I just wanted to sit and talk to her. I wanted to know everything about her. She had an inward beauty I had not known. When she smiled, her eyes sparkled and her face and body glowed with happiness. "Have you been here long?" I asked.

"Oh yes, I have been here since the beginning of time. Long before you were born on earth."

She then asked if I would like to hear her story. Of course, I couldn't wait to hear about her life. I listened closely as she began.

"My life began a very long time ago. Let me tell you of the very first person God brought to life. Long before I existed, God created a perfect man. The man was conceived from the dust of the ground. God just picked up some red soil from the top layer of the earth's surface, and, in his hands, he molded and fashioned a human being into the very image of himself. God then breathed life into the man's nostrils. And instantly this man, whom God called Adam, became the first living being on earth.

"God set Adam in a place called paradise and gave Adam complete authority over all the land and everything in the land, including the animals.

"Adam loved this land called paradise and all the animals God created for him. But as time went on, God felt Adam should have another human being to share his world with him. Every time God had created something, he always whispered, 'It is good.' But as he watched Adam talking to the animals and not having a soul mate for himself, God said, 'This is not good.' He knew it would be better if Adam had a wife to share in his happiness. So God did something remarkable. The Lord God caused Adam to fall into a deep sleep. When Adam was sound asleep, God put his hand into Adam's left side and took a rib right out of Adam's body. And from that rib, God fashioned a perfect woman. I was that woman! When Adam woke up, he was delighted. My husband thanked the Lord God for me and said, 'This is my wife, bone of my bone, and flesh of my flesh.'

"It was love at first sight for both of us. We were completely happy with one another living in this wonderful paradise with God. We were victorious residents of a beautiful and perfect world. We could not have asked for anything more.

"Flowing through the middle of our paradise was an extraordinary river that gave nourishment to all of the plants and animals. Splendid flowers and bountiful trees were at our command. Plants produced delicious fruit to eat if we desired. Everywhere we went and everything we did, God was there to support us. Day after day, we experienced God's magnificence in all of his glory.

"Our original assignment was to watch over God's creation with unquestioning trust. You might say that Adam and I were God's first gardeners. We never did work too hard because the animals were very eager to help. We would laugh as the wolves started digging holes to plant seeds. Adam and I would then place the seed into the hole. It was the lions next. They would stand with their tails close to the space that had the seed and then push the soil with their big back paws until the space was filled. The elephants were always standing by with their trunks filled and waiting patiently to hose down a stream of cool water on us as well as the newly planted seeds. We enjoyed the planting season almost as much as the harvest.

"In the center of our magnificent garden stood a very large tree. God called this tree the Tree of Knowledge of Good and Evil. This was the only tree in all of the land that God commanded Adam and I not to touch.

"It was a day much like today that I decided to take a walk through paradise. I had never been very close to the tree, and I thought it very interesting that God didn't want Adam or I to touch it. As I approached the heart of the garden, I started walking more rapidly. It seemed there was a current of air pulling me. Faster and faster I went. Unexpected anticipation of seeing the tree was growing inside of me. When I reached the base of the tree, I was astonished at its size. It was breathtaking. The area around the tree was over a hundred feet, and it stood far above the other trees in height. Small branches extending from larger branches were heavy with huge golden apples. The watery skin of the tree seemed to breathe in air every second.

"Performing at the highest point of the tree, I could see angels. They were exquisite. I could hear their voices singing holy and mighty is our God. It was as if they were guarding the tree from harm. I wondered how harm could come to a perfect tree in a perfect world. Now for the first time I knew what made this tree different from the others. This Tree of Knowledge of Good and Evil was endowed with powers for spiritual healing. The fully developed roots, carefully concealed since the beginning of time, had been supported in a foundation of love. Divided and separated but brought together by one loving sovereign provider, the branches were established in the truthfulness of God and held the life story of every human being. Together these branches made a royal crown as they reached upward.

"The tree's golden apples were gifts of peace, prosperity, and acts of kindness from the Lord. The Tree of Knowledge of Good and Evil represented God's love for all humanity.

"As I stood absorbed in the splendor of the tree, a handsome serpent approached me. He was probably the most magnificent of all God's creatures. He was stately and forceful and stood upright looking at me as if he understood what was in my mind. When he spoke to me, his words were plain and almost magical. He looked directly in my face as he said, 'This is certainly the most beautiful of all the trees in the garden. I can assure you the golden apples have a delicious taste.'

"I answered him, 'Yes, it is extraordinary. I can see the heart of the apple through its clear golden covering.' The Lord told me not to touch the tree. If I did I would surely die.

"He started mocking me. 'Do you really believe God would give to you and Adam all that is in this beautiful place only to not allow you to touch the golden apples? You know how much he loves you. Why would God not let you enjoy one golden apple?'

"I thought about what the serpent had said and decided to ignore him. Now I had seen the tree for what it really was and knew I should obey the Lord.

"Immediately, the serpent realized I was ignoring him, and he started laughing as he said, 'You know that if you eat from this tree you will be like God. You will gain knowledge, and the understanding will improve your life.'

"I pretended not to hear him. Then he came closer and began to whisper, 'I would not lie to you. You will be a god!'

"He sounded so sure of himself. Maybe it was true; maybe I could have just one golden apple.

"During those years of walking with God, Adam and I never once thought of the consequence for disobedience. And then, in a moment of greed, I made the decision to disobey the word of God. I reached up and put my hand on one of the beautiful golden apples. As soon as I touched it, I knew in my heart it was wrong. But it was too late. That ugly serpent, that minutes before I thought was so handsome, was partially right, because immediately I knew the difference between good and evil.

"I would always be known as the wife of Adam, but now I would also be known as the first person to disobey the word of God. It was then I realized I was naked. I took a fig leaf from a nearby tree and pulled on it until it came loose. I covered my body with it, but even this did not help the shame I felt. I called out for Adam. As soon as Adam saw I was hiding my body, he knew something was wrong. 'Eve, why do you have that fig leaf over you?'

"'Never mind that,' I said. 'Come and taste this delicious fruit. At first Adam resisted, but I kept on talking until I finally convinced him to take a bite of the forbidden fruit. I didn't want to be alone in my sin.

"That was the beginning of a new relationship with God. It was also the very moment that time began on earth.

"Adam took some fig leaves and covered his body and told me God would be angry with us for our disobedience. I had never seen an expression of fear before, but somehow I knew and felt the same emotion he was feeling. Adam's voice cracked as he spoke, 'Eve, we must try to find a secret place.'

"We had just found a hiding place under a shrub with thick green branches when we heard God. His voice was strong and loud.

"'Adam, Eve, come out of your secret place. Do you think you can conceal yourselves from me? Tell me, what is it that makes you uncomfortable?'

"We knew God knew what we had done. He wanted us to acknowledge our sin to him. Shamefully, we kept our heads and eyes downward so we didn't have to look at him, and we began to speak softly as we told him what he already knew.

"God listened, and, without giving a lecture on our disobedience, he simply said, 'Woman, because you did not value my authority, you will experience sorrow as you bear many children in the years to come. Adam, because you have listened to your wife and have disobeyed me, I will curse the earth. There will be thorns and weeds, and you will work by the sweat of your brow until the day you return to the earth from which you were formed. From this day forward, until the day comes when you will surely die, you will not forget your transgression.'

"It may seem odd, but at the time I did wonder, *What is a thorn and what are weeds?* Then something extraordinary happened. When he finished speaking, God picked up a lamb that was standing nearby. First, he put the animal to death, and from this blameless animal, God made a covering for both Adam and I. We were given a blessing of mercy and wrapped with the sacrifice of the innocent lamb. Then God sent us away from the garden forever. It was on this day that the mouths of all the animals were closed so they could no longer speak.

"God then placed a great sword at the entrance of the garden. It had fire coming from it as it spun around and around so the flames of the sword were flying in every direction. Cherubim were placed at the east end of the garden to guard the way to the Tree of Knowledge of Good and Evil. No one would enter this enchanting safe world again.

"From that time until our death on earth, Adam and I lived in the land of Elda. It was there I learned what these things called weeds and thorns were all about. Sin had entered into our hearts, and now we called upon God to forgive us our transgression. Our hearts were heavy, and we didn't know God had already forgiven our sin. We made a raised altar on which we burned frankincense and myrrh spices as an offering to God. The Lord breathed in the sweet aroma of our offering, and, in his never-ending mercy, he had compassion on us. He told Adam and me that one day our physical bodies would return to the earth from which he formed us and we would receive new spiritual bodies and live forever in a place called heaven. I asked God, 'How can we once again have fellowship with you, Lord?'

"Then he told us of his plan. 'Remember when I slaughtered the lamb to make a covering for you both? That was a representation of my son, Jesus Christ, who will be put to death for the redemption of all mankind. One day, my son, Jesus, will freely come as the Lamb of God. He will be born of a virgin through the power of the Holy Spirit. He will walk earth preaching and teaching my word. My son will heal the sick; he will give courage to those who are broken with fear and hope to all of those in despair. At the age of thirty-three, my son will be accused of blasphemy. One of his followers will betray him with a kiss, and he will be given over to the governor of Rome. Jesus will be bruised for your iniquities, and he will be crushed for your transgressions. Near the city gate, just beyond Jerusalem's northern wall, my son's hands and feet will be nailed to a wooden cross. A sword will pierce his side, and a wreath of thorns will crush his skull. Above his head, a sign will be placed, *Jesus of Nazareth, King of the Jews.* His blood will spill to the ground to cover the sin of the world. My only son, Jesus Christ, will hang on a cross on Mount Calvary for three agonizing hours, and after this, his suffering will end. The sky will light up, the earth will crack, and he will cry out, "It is finished." That is the exact moment that Satan and sin will be defeated forever. There will be great rejoicing, for Jesus triumphs over his death. I will lift up my son, Jesus Christ, on the third day after his crucifixion, and he will ascend to heaven and once again remain with me forever.

"'Only through the blood of the Lamb of God can your sin be forever forgotten. Your offering of spices was pleasing, but it was not sufficient. There is no promise of redemption except through the blood of my only begotten Son. By faith, you enter into our presence by accepting the sacrifice of my Son. If you do this, the blood of the Lamb of God will protect you and keep you alive forever.

"'My Son and I love you with perfect love. We agreed that you are worth the price of our suffering. We will be waiting for you at the throne room in heaven.'"

Eve finished her story. "Adam and I accepted God's offer, and that is why I was received into the arms of Jesus, just as you were."

When she finished, I said to her, "That is the most wonderful story I have ever heard. Thank you, Eve, for sharing your experience. Isn't it wonderful how God made a way for you and Adam?"

And she answered, "Yes, heaven is all about the grace of God. It is a choice that God has given to each individual since the beginning of time. In the book of John, in the fourteenth chapter, a man by the name of Thomas asked the Lord how he could know the way to heaven, and Jesus answered him, 'I am the way, the truth, and the life; no man or woman or child cometh unto the Father, but by me."

Eldon seemed to come from nowhere. "Lynne, it's time for me to give your assignment to Gabriel. Your story will bring comfort to those on earth who have lost their loved ones and wonder what became of them."

I placed my beautiful journal in Eldon's hand. "I pray my story will bring comfort, happiness, and peace to those who have not yet entered heaven."

This story never ends, because eternity never ends. This was just my first assignment here. I can hardly wait until my next. There is abundant peace here in heaven, and this wonderful land of wonder will be here forever and ever. What I have told you is just the start of my new life, and I will never cease to marvel at the start of a new day. God is forever revealing himself to us in new and wondrous ways.

There are always new places to discover and new people to meet. Some have been here for a very long time, and others arrive each new day. Heaven is a big place, and I know it will take me a very long time to visit the many towns and cities and the wonderful people who live here. And that's okay, because this is just the beginning.

It is a bright and beautiful Sunday morning on earth, and as I peek down through the clouds, I can see Mama. She no longer cries all the time. Today she looks in high spirits as she reads the Word of God.

Sometimes I think she knows when I'm watching her. She gets that look on her face, and good thoughts enter into her mind. And then I hear her say, "Thank you, God."

Today she read the book of Revelation, and God told her one day she too will enter through the welcome gate. Mama is content for now because she knows the day will come when she will have the privilege of holding her Lynne and Johnny in her arms once again. For now, she will hold us in her heart, and she will keep busy, doing what God has for her on earth. God has given her my brothers, Joe and Kevin, and my sisters, Carol Ann and Jeanne, and nine wonderful grandchildren to hold and to love while they enjoy life on earth. She understands no matter where a person resides, heaven or earth, God has a job for them to do. And until her time comes, when the angels escort her to heaven, she will continue to praise and thank God that two of her beautiful children were especially chosen to reside with the King.

I had no idea I was on my way to heaven that October afternoon. Someday soon the angels will either escort you to the pearly gates or you will witness his coming in the clouds. I hope you will be ready.

And when the time comes, stop by for a visit. Ask anyone and they will give you directions to my place at 7 Romans Road, just across from Proverbs Avenue in the city of Isaiah, in the kingdom of God, on his magnificent planet in his spectacular universe.